Nashville Heat

Bethany Michaels

Nashville Heat

Copyright © 2009 by Bethany Michaels

Ravenous Romance™
100 Cummings Center
Suite 125G
Beverly, MA 01915

A version of this work was previously published in electronic form by Ravenous Romance.

ISBN-13-978-1-60777-640-6

This book is a work of fiction, and any resemblance to persons living or dead is purely coincidental.

Chapter One

THE FIRST time I saw Dex Wilder, I was wearing a bed sheet and body glitter and serving *hors d'oeuvres* on the lawn in front of the world's only full-scale replica of the Parthenon.

The party was hosted by one of Nashville's numerous record labels. I, along with the rest of wait staff, was supposed to resemble a Greek goddess, serving record company executives, music publishers, promoters, country music radio station VIPs, retail music buyers, established artists with the label, selected newcomers and assorted hangers-on. Those were mostly girls with short skirts and surgically enhanced tops.

What I actually looked like was a toga-party call girl. My honey-blond hair had been coaxed into cascading ringlets. My skin, mostly bare above the top of the toga that showed more cleavage than I was comfortable with, was spattered in gold glitter. My makeup had been applied with a heavy hand by my new roommate. Dark eyeliner ringed my light blue eyes and thick mascara caked my already black lashes. I'd drawn the line at the lipstick Becca had tried to slather over my lips, though. I hated the stuff and had gone with cherry Chapstick instead.

I found it hard to believe Greeks ever looked like I did, given the fact they used public baths and propane curling irons hadn't been invented yet, but whatever. It was a paying job and since I'd been in Nashville only a couple of weeks, I needed the cash. Badly.

I was on the lookout for some of the country music stars I'd idolized all through my teen years, stars who had inspired me to leave my small Indiana hometown and venture south in the first place. Everywhere I went, from seedy bars where I'd played one gig so far with a couple of so-so guitar players, to the Walmart on the south side, I kept my eyes open.

The catering gig was no star-making venture, but it afforded me the chance to rub elbows with Nashville's music community, even if I was mostly cleaning up half-eaten food and tepid glasses of champagne. As menial as it seemed, it was still Nashville. And that was good enough for me.

The Parthenon soiree had netted a few notable sightings, and I had fantasies of a chance meeting leading to a record deal and instant stardom. That was the way it happened in all the *E! True Hollywood Stories*. So I was serving my crab cakes and indulging in a little fan-girl surveillance on that warm summer night when a man I didn't recognize touched my arm.

"Ma'am?"

It was just one word, but in his fluid tenor and down home sexy Southern drawl, that was all it took.

I turned and looked up at him.

I'm tall, about five feet, ten inches, and this guy was a good five inches taller. He had deep blue eyes that were very slightly crinkled at the corners, straight white teeth, and a pair of soft-looking lips that were formed into a slightly crooked smile. With the black cowboy hat and hint of black beard stubble, he was every cowboy fantasy I'd ever entertained come to life. Only hotter.

"Ma'am?" he said again, still grinning at me.

The silver tray I was balancing on one hand tilted to the side, and I caught it just before half-eaten *hors d'oeuvres*, dirty cocktail napkins and a jumble of glassware crashed to the ground at the pointed tips of his shiny black boots.

"Yes?" I finally managed.

"Do you think I could get a beer?" He held up his flute of Korbel. "I can't stand this sweet stuff."

He was still smiling.

I was still staring.

"Um, I can check with Ricky. He's the owner. I'll, um, check."

"Thank you, ma'am," he said. His straight white teeth gleamed in the soft light cast by the strings of white lights crisscrossing the outdoor shindig. He set his untouched glass of champagne on my tray. "I'll wait right here."

Sometimes you meet someone for the first time and the attraction is so swift and undeniable that it takes your breath away. There's a sort of immediate awareness, an invisible but unequivocal pull, and your whole world shifts slightly on its axis. Your heart beats a desperate staccato and the blood rushes fiercely through your veins. You can't speak. You can't think. You can't breathe.

That's the way it was when I met Dex.

I don't know if love at first sight exists, but lust at first sight, instant infatuation, sure as hell does.

I smiled up at him, or tried to, and made my way through the crowd to the building's north side, where my boss had set up his command post. Turning to look over my shoulder before I disappeared around the corner of the building, I found the cowboy still staring after me with that crooked grin on his face. I could feel his gaze almost like a caress and my body temperature went up a few degrees.

"Oh my God," my new roommate, Becca, gushed as soon as I set my tray down on the folding table at command central. "Did you see that guy?"

I didn't have to ask which guy. There was only one, now.

I managed a quick nod. "He wants a beer."

I tightened my toga, which had begun to wilt in the humid June air, and wiped a bead of sweat from between my braless breasts. The breeze felt good. It was a warm night but I wasn't all that sure my burning skin had anything to do with ambient temperature.

"Damn rednecks," grumbled my boss, Ricky Moon. "Always with the beer." He pulled out a metal washtub of ice filled with longnecks. "It took some doin' to get my hands on enough Korbel for these jerks and now all they want is Bud Light."

Ricky had been a struggling musician back in the day and had found catering a way to supplement his meager music income. Now he did it full time, his dreams of music stardom replaced with dreams of a successful business and a steady living. Despite his balding pate, the belly that had seen just a few too many beers, and despite his complaints and a constant stream of profanity that would do any sailor proud, Ricky was a good guy with a soft spot for young struggling musical types. He let people off without too much complaint if a sudden opportunity to gig at a local club presented itself and always had a gruff but encouraging word for all of us.

I plucked two beers out of the ice and put them on my tray with a couple of clean pilsner glasses. Ricky handed me a fancy silver bottle opener with another comment under his breath about those "damn rednecks" while Becca reloaded her platter with Greek-themed *hors d'oeuvres* from warming trays and we headed back out to the party.

Becca and I were total opposites in looks. I was tall and fair with blond hair and blue eys, while she was dark, with beautiful shiny hair the color of dark chocolate, luminous dark brown eyes that tilted up just slightly at the corners. She had a full mouth and was never without her fire-engine red lipstick. Becca was calm, confident, and exuded sensuality with every gesture.

"Hey, there's your cowboy," she whispered when we rounded the side of the building. "I heard he just signed with Red Wolf

Records. He's their new golden boy." Becca tugged the neck of her toga lower to show even more of cleavage.

"If they put his picture on the cover of his album, it'll go platinum inside of a week." I tucked a loose curl behind my ear and made my way carefully down the steep Parthenon steps in my rented goddess-gold sandals. "What's his name?"

Becca smiled. "Dex Wilder."

"Seriously?"

"Yeah. Yummy, huh?" We parted ways at the bottom of the steps. "See if you can get his phone number. We can share." Becca winked and headed towards a group of suits seated at a small round table in the conspicuous center of the gathering.

I took a deep breath, straightened my shoulders and headed towards where I'd left the hot cowboy. Dex.

The alcohol was flowing and the crowd was enjoying the party. People were up and about, mingling, schmoozing, and kissing up whenever possible. It was crowded and I was jostled a bit, but I knew where I'd left Dex and headed in that direction.

All of a sudden, the proverbial crowd parted and there he was. He should have had a spotlight on him and some soaring instrumental theme playing in the background; he was that good looking. I stumbled slightly but made my way to him, drawn like a magnet to a big hunk of metal. A really big hunk.

He was holding a plate of *hors d'oeuvres* in one hand. "You found one," he said, taking one of the longnecks from my tray. He popped the cap with his thumb and took a long draw from the bottle, ignoring the glasses I'd also brought. I watched his throat move as he swallowed and wondered what he would do if I went up on my tiptoes and pressed a kiss or two right on that Adam's apple.

His eyes never left mine as he drank and when he lowered the bottle, he ran the back of his hand over his lips and grinned down at me.

"Thanks."

"You're welcome." I started to move on through the crowd, hoping my feet would obey my will, when he put his hand on my arm again.

"I was hoping maybe you could tell me what these are." He held up his plate. "I don't know my way around all this frou-frou stuff. Like this. Looks like toast to me."

"Shrimp bruschetta."

He flashed that sexy grin and my knees went weak. "I knew you were the woman for the job. How about this lettuce thing?"

"That's dolma. Rice, lamb and onion with olive oil and lemon, wrapped in a grape leaf. And the green balls are feta cheese truffles coated in parsley."

"And I'm guessing these ain't onion rings?"

I shook my head. "Fried calamari."

"Cala-what?"

"Calamari. Squid."

"Ugh. No thanks. What ever happened to buffalo wings and crab cakes?"

"It's really good, actually. Tastes like chicken. Try it."

"No way. I don't eat anything with tentacles."

"Coward."

He narrowed his eyes on me, but was still smiling. "You first."

"Can't. I'm on duty."

"I won't tell anybody. Here." Dex plucked a golden ring from his plate and held it to my lips.

It was a dare, and looking into his deep blue eyes and teasing grin, I couldn't resist. I stuck my tongue through the hole and pulled the fried ring into my mouth. The calamari wasn't as hot as it could be, but it wasn't bad for catering.

"See? Delicious." I grabbed a napkin from my tray and patted my mouth. "As long as you don't get a head."

Dex eyed the platter suspiciously. "I don't think so."

"Come on. You promised." I chose a smaller ring and held it to his lips as he had done to me.

Leaning in, Dex held my gaze and sucked the whole ring and the tips of my fingers into his warm, wet mouth.

I shivered, despite the heat.

Dex pulled back slowly, chewing the fish.

"Not bad," he said. "Kind of spongy." He took a swig of beer. "But I'm still partial to a good batch of burn-your-tongue-off buffalo wings."

"Don't let my boss hear you say that. He'll pop something."

"It'll be our secret, then." He traded his empty bottle for the full one on my tray. "So. Do you come here often?"

I laughed at that. "Don't you have any better lines than that?" As if he would need them.

He took another pull on the bottle. "No, ma'am. I don't."

"Well, I'm an expert," I said. "How about 'I lost my phone number. Can I have yours?'"

He nodded. "Not half bad. Think that will work?"

"Maybe. It's all in the delivery."

"Hey, I remember one that worked in college: 'Hi. I'm Mr. Right. I hear you've been looking for me.'"

I groaned. "No."

"Hmm. Didn't like that one, huh?" He drained his beer and put the bottle on my tray.

I shook my head. "You need to work on that."

"So what are you doing later?"

"Ugh, that's the worst," I said, laughing now.

He didn't return my laugh. Instead he stepped closer. "No, I mean, what are you doing later? After the party." He looked down into my eyes and the heat that had sparked between us ignited a full-blown blaze.

His chest brushed my breasts and I could feel the heat of him, the scent of his subtle aftershave, and warmth instantly began to pool in my belly. I could so imagine bringing this cowboy home.

It was tempting, but....

"I'm going home," I said. "Alone." I smiled. "Sorry."

He looked a little disappointed. I imagined he didn't get turned down very much. "Can I get your number, at least?"

"Sure." I smiled and turned over a cocktail napkin to write on. "Give me your pen."

"I didn't bring one."

"You were never a Boy Scout, were you?" I teased.

"Well, I wasn't expecting to meet a goddess tonight." He grinned and stroked my bare arm. "How about I hunt down something to write with and find you later?"

"Okay," I said, biting my lip. He was hot and just the thought of his calling me, hearing that voice saying naughty things to me in that sexy Southern drawl of his….

Despite my body's reaction to Dex, I knew he was a distraction I couldn't afford. I had moved to Nashville against my family's wishes and with their smug assurance that I'd be back when the money ran out. I was determined to prove them wrong. I needed to focus on my career, not a boyfriend. I was nuts to take this, whatever it was, anywhere beyond flirtation. But boy, he was persuasive, especially when he looked down at me like he wanted to eat me up. Okay, so I was weak. At least where Dex Wilder was concerned.

"Later, then," I said.

Someone called his name, and a man in an expensive suit threw a semi-drunk arm around his shoulders, or tried to. The man was good foot shorter than Dex.

"Later." Dex winked at me and let the man lead him through the crowd.

I spent the next three hours serving champagne and *hors d'oeuvres*, fending off the occasional squeeze and pick-up line with a smile and a clever line, and before I knew it, the crowd had thinned and it was time to start packing up.

I looked around but didn't see Dex. I was sure he'd already left, probably with one of the record execs and their entourage of bimbos in one of the white stretch limos parked along the lighted drive.

Oh, well. It was better this way. Flirting with Dex had been fun and I was sure it was his smile, his eyes, his scent that would keep me awake most of the night. But that was as far as it would go.

The tips had been good, the company relatively tame. No fist fights or food poisoning. It was a good night in the catering business and I was ready to head home.

I helped Ricky and the others stack the dirty dishes in tubs and load them into the white catering van emblazoned with Blue Moon Catering.

"So did you get his number?" Becca asked, handing Ricky the final load of dirty glasses.

"No."

"Bummer. He's a hottie. Maybe he'll be at the Frist party next week, though."

"I pay you to serve the drinks, not pick up the guests," Ricky grumbled, wiping his hands on a dish towel.

"Sure, Ricky," Becca said, a perfectly innocent look painted across her face. "That would be against the rules."

Ricky grunted and closed the doors to the van.

"Be at the museum at seven o' clock sharp. And don't forget to return those," he said gesturing at the togas. "It's that place down on Church Street. Don't forget the deposit."

"Will do, boss," Becca said, giving him a mock salute.

Ricky rolled his eyes. "You girls need a ride or anything?"

No matter how tough he acted, Ricky still watched out for us in true Southern gentleman style.

"No, thanks," I said. "I have my car."

"Okay. See you Tuesday, then." Ricky climbed in the van and pulled away.

"I'm beat. Let's get going," I said to Becca.

"Thanks, but I've got a ride." Becca glanced at a good-looking blond cowboy who had appeared around the side of the building as soon as Ricky left. He wore the look of a guy about to get lucky. "Don't wait up."

She patted her hair and walked with an exaggerated sway in her hips over to the guy. He put his arm around her and they went off together into the shadows.

I rolled my eyes and started towards my car.

Becca. She was great roommate so far in that she'd paid the first month's rent and didn't drink all my Diet Coke. And she was out more nights than not, so I basically had our tiny two-bedroom apartment overlooking Broadway all to myself.

She had a great voice and could play any tune on the piano by ear, but I worried that her pursuits of the carnal variety might start to affect her career goals.

I sat down on the stairs of the Parthenon and slipped off the cheap, ill-fitting sandals. My feet were sore and it felt good to stretch my toes. I didn't make a habit of hanging out in the park at night, but it was a nice night, now that the sweltering heat and humidity of the summer day had faded with the sunset. Spotlights on all sides of the Parthenon lit up the building like it was midday and the Park Police were wandering around somewhere, so I figured I was safe enough for a few minutes.

The concrete of the steps still held the warmth of the day and for a moment, I just sat there, enjoying the night. Birds chirped out their goodnights to one another from the trees, and the gurgle of the fountain in the center of the small lake soothed my nerves. A light breeze cooled my skin and brought the rich scent of lush green vegetation to my nostrils. But still, I couldn't help thinking about a certain cowboy.

That's when I heard his voice.

"I bet you thought I forgot about you, huh?"

He stepped out of the shadows, his thumbs tucked in the front pockets of his tight jeans and looked at me from under the brim of his black cowboy hat, pulled low.

I wanted to say something witty. Something sexy. Something to make such a gorgeous, charismatic guy remember me forever. I swallowed.

"Hi."

He climbed the steep steps and sat down beside me. "Waiting on a ride?"

There was a scant inch between his body and mine and heat radiated from him like I was sitting next to an inferno.

"No, just relaxing a minute before I head home."

"Mind if I sit with you?"

"No. Not at all."

Silent tension built between us like the charge in the air just before a lightning strike. It was his scent, his body heat, the night, his closeness. It was the anticipation. The danger. The pure animal attraction that hummed between us.

"So what do you do when you're not being a goddess?" He turned towards me.

"I'm a singer." I smiled. "Like of half of Nashville."

"Have I seen you anywhere?"

"Not unless you hang out at Willie's Wagon Wheel."

He laughed again. "It's been a while, but I've tossed down a few over there. I played there a few times, too. Watch out for Willie, though."

"Yeah. Thanks for the warning." I'd slapped Willie's roaming hands more than once while the band and I were setting up and tearing down the previous night.

Dex laughed. "He has a thing for blondes. Can't say that I blame him." He leaned closer and, still smiling, tucked a loose corkscrew of hair behind my ear.

That simple touch, barely a whisper of skin on skin, seemed to ignite something in both of us. The thing that had been between us all night, barely under control. Carnal awareness had burgeoned from that first "Ma'am" but when his finger brushed my cheekbone and then the shell of my ear, well, it simply exploded.

I tilted my head back and swayed towards him at the same time he reached to cup my face in his hands. Our lips met in a sizzle of heat and need that took my breath away.

His lips were warm and probably would have been soft if he hadn't kissed me so hard and with so much built-up tension. His tongue did funny, fantastic things to my mouth and he nibbled and kissed and caressed my mouth so thoroughly that I instantly knew what sex with him would be like: hot, hard, and devastating.

The leash on my control had snapped, too. I slid my hands in his hair, knocking his hat to the cement, and pressed against every inch of him I could reach. He tasted a little of beer and something sweet. The slight scruff on his cheeks and chin tickled my mouth and face and I grew even hotter imagining that whisker burn all over my body.

He broke the kiss and with a wild look in his eyes, he pulled me to standing and walked us backwards until the warm, smooth stone of the building was at my back. With the spotlights shining on us, I could see the way his eyes darkened with need, the set of his jaw, the pulse point in his neck and the way his breath came swift and strong from between his white teeth.

Dex slid his arms around my waist and lower until he could squeeze my backside, pulling me against his body. I could feel how much he wanted me, too, and fire shot straight to my center.

He kissed a trail down the side of my neck and throat and I looked skyward to give him better access. One of his thighs slipped between mine to provide the intimate pressure I needed. I bit my lip, loving the hot, sweet need that coursed through my veins.

Dex moved lower and pressed hungry kisses along the neckline of my toga. He tugged the loose top lower and explored the exposed flesh with tongue and lips until I groaned his name.

I felt him smile and he broke off long enough to look at me, his lips wet, his eyes large and dark with desire. "Say my name."

"Dex," I whispered again. "Dex."

He groaned and slipped the fabric of my toga down my arm. The sensation of warm night air on one bare breast followed by the sweep of his tongue and rough pull of his lips brought a renewed chorus of his name from my lips.

I let my hands roam over his broad shoulders, down the snug fit of his shirt. I pushed it up a little so I could feel him, flesh to flesh. His skin was hot and smooth and I wanted to feel that hard body against mine. I wanted to feel him over me and inside me and hear his deep voice tell me exactly what he was going to do to me all night long.

Desire blazed through me fast and strong. Tension wound tight in my belly and moisture gathered between my thighs. I gritted my teeth. I wanted him fast and hard and right now.

I tugged at his large belt buckle until it came loose, then fumbled with the button on his Levi's. His state made it difficult, so he pushed my hands aside and eased it carefully down himself.

When he was free, I grasped his burning flesh and, licking my lips, stroked him from root to tip. His hips jerked against mine and he tugged the skirt of my toga up with shaking hands until the night air kissed my bare legs and thighs.

We were going to do it. Right here, right now. Neither of us had enough patience to go back to my apartment or his, or even make it to my car. The forbidden fantasy of sex in a public place amped up my already fierce libido to a point of near pain. But I knew we were on display under the spotlights that lit up the building. And the Park Police were out there somewhere.

"The light," I managed to get out, almost too lost to care. "We should probably go –"

He broke away from me and before I knew what he had in mind, he kicked out the spotlight. A shower of glass and sparks exploded from the box and then we were alone in darkness.

He strode back to me and buried his hands in my hair. Dex pressed against me so I could feel every hard plane of his body. "Better?" he asked and even though it was now dark, I could feel my favorite bad-boy grin stretch across his lips.

"Perfect," I sad just before his mouth came down over mine again.

Dex wasted no time. He shoved the toga up to my waist to stroke me though the silk of my red thong. I would have been a puddle at his feet if he hadn't been pressing me into the wall, holding me upright.

I ran my hands under his shirt, over his chest, teasing his flat nipples until they were as peaked as mine. Then I let my hands wander down, down, down to his hips and pulled him even harder against me. I wanted him, needed to feel him.

His fingers traced the line of my panties before delving inside. He stroked me gently, but with just enough pressure to make me cry out. Tension built low in my belly and the blood rushed though my veins. I arched against him.

"Dex." It was a cry, a plea, and he understood implicitly what I needed.

One long finger slid deep inside me and my legs buckled. He grasped me around the waist and moved his mouth to my ear. "You're so sexy, so ready for me, aren't you, honey? You're making me crazy."

When he added a second finger and began to move slowly in and out, I couldn't speak, could barely breathe. The pressure, the long stretch felt so good. It had been a long time, and Dex Wilder was definitely better than anything I could have imagined.

Just when I was ready to start begging, he withdrew. He tugged my panties off and he hitched my leg up over his hip.

I heard the jingle of his belt buckle and felt him slip his jeans down a little while he fumbled in his wallet for protection.

It was crazy. Pure crazy, I thought from somewhere within the sensual spell Dex had cast over me. I didn't do things like this. I never hooked up with random guys, never brought guys home whom I hadn't dated for at least a month, and I never went to bed with a guy on the first date.

But all those little rules of conduct had nothing to do with what was between Dex and me right at that moment. It was beyond reason, beyond rules. It was a purely carnal, spontaneous thing. Which is what made it so perfect.

When Dex was ready, he wasted no more time.

"Hold on to me, baby." He grasped my backside in his large hands and, hooking my other leg over his hip, slid inside me in one long, smooth stroke.

If his fingers drove me to the edge of insanity, the rest of him pushed me right over the edge. He rotated his hips and did sort of a slow swivel-thrust thing that had me panting and gritting my teeth, wanting more.

But he kept his slow, teasing rhythm, sliding almost all the way out before thrusting inside once more in a long, slow glide. He put his mouth on my neck. He kissed me, nipped lightly, then traced the nibble with his tongue.

I grasped his shoulders, nails digging in. His big hands cradled my backside, squeezing and stroking and bringing me up to meet him.

The tension coiling within me was unbearable. I was hot and aching everywhere, it seemed, and every nerve was on edge.

Waiting, wanting. He brought me closer and closer to the edge with his maddening slowness. But I wanted him wild. I wanted him to slam into me harder and harder until I exploded.

I pitched forward and threw my arms around his neck, taking control of the kiss. I bit at his neck and pressed hot, hard kisses there. I nipped at his ear, tugged at his hair. Finally I pushed him beyond his control.

He thrust forward hard and slammed me against the wall. His rhythm increased as he pounded unto me harder, driving deeper. He grunted with the effort, low in his throat.

"Yes," I breathed, my eyes closed. "Yes. Harder."

He complied and drove into me mercilessly. The stone scraped at my flesh but the slight burning sensation only added to the frenzy and before long, the tension had gathered into one big knot. My breath hitched and then everything burst in waves of pleasure so hard and strong that I forgot to breathe.

I felt him stiffen, then groan long and low. His breath was ragged in my ear and I gripped his damp hair as the last quivers of pleasure wracked my body.

When the shudders subsided, he pulled his head back, and even though it was dark, I could hear the smile in his passion-husky voice.

"You're the hottest thing I've ever seen."

I grinned. "So are you."

He withdrew and released my legs.

My toga fell back into place, covering me, I tugged my top back into place. I didn't know where my panties were.

Dex took care of the condom and tugged his jeans back up just before a beam of light illuminated us.

"Evenin', folks." The officer squatted in front of the light Dex had kicked out. He plucked a piece of glass out of the lawn and held it up in front of the flashlight's piercing beam.

"You know what happened here?"

"Uh…"

"Kids," I said quickly. "I saw some kids up here a while ago." I shot Dex a look. I could tell he was uncomfortable with the fib, but he didn't argue.

The guard grunted and got to his feet. "Kids," he said. "Get a look at any of them?"

I shook my head. "Not really. I think one of them was wearing a Vandy hat, though." Vanderbilt University was just on the other side of West End Avenue and I was sure, at one time or another, some student had gotten drunk and kicked out the floodlights. Maybe for the same reason Dex had.

"The park closes in a few minutes, folks. You'll have to get going."

I nodded. "Of course. Thanks, Officer. Um, good luck finding those hooligans."

Dex walked me back to my car, holding my hand and carrying my bag. Somehow, that innocent touch was more intimate than sex and it made me uncomfortable. Now that the rush of gotta-have-it-now lust has passed, it was a little awkward. I couldn't help but wonder what he must think of me. Did he think I did this every day? That I was a slut? And more disturbingly, why did I care what he thought?

I unlocked my beat-up Toyota and he leaned against me, pressing me into the cold metal for a long, deep, slow kiss. The urgency was gone, but desire still simmered just below the surface. I knew that if I let it go on, he'd be suggesting we to go to his place or mine. This was uncomfortable enough. I couldn't imagine what a morning after would be like. Mortifying.

I pulled back and pressed both hands to his chest, trying to give myself a little distance. He leaned back.

"I have to go," I said, not quite meeting his eye. "I…have an early appointment." The only appointment I had was with a huge cup of coffee and the morning paper, but what was one more fib?

"Oh. Okay." He seemed surprised but recovered quickly.

I opened the door to the car, and threw my bag inside before sliding into the driver's seat.

He leaned down, resting his arm on the open door and gave me another hot kiss.

"Can I call you?" he asked with the smile that was sure to break hearts. And sell albums.

I started the car. "This has been great, Dex. Really great. But let's just let it go at that, okay?"

I tugged the door and he stepped back.

"But –"

I couldn't look him in the eye. He seemed so disappointed. But I was sure with his upcoming album release and all the groupies it would bring, he'd forget about me in no time. I could get back to concentrating on building a career and he could concentrate on – whatever he wanted.

"I really have to go." I smiled brightly. "Take care. Good luck with the album."

I pulled away before he could say anything else, but I couldn't help but look in the rearview. He was standing where I'd left him, staring after me.

* * * *

That was almost two years ago. Before he was on the cover of every country music magazine in existence. Before the certified double-platinum debut album. Before the *Playboy* interview, the *Rolling Stone* cover, the CMA awards and the title of Sexiest Man Alive.

Everywhere I turned, there he was, smiling at me, and it brought back in vivid detail our night together.

From the tabloid photos that surfaced at least every other minute, he'd forgotten me. Whether he was hanging out after a concert or tearing it up at some Hollywood party, scantily-clad girls were the staple. He looked like he was having the time of his life and I was sure that one summer night in Nashville wasn't even a blip on his radar.

I'd tried to forget, too. Tried to forget the casual way he'd brushed the hair from my face. The way he'd grinned at me with a light of mischief burning in his ocean blue eyes. The way his jeans hugged his buff body and the tilt of his cowboy hat had sent my heart into an unnatural rhythm. The way he'd felt when we were together. The way he'd looked at me with tenderness and longing as I'd left him afterwards.

But I hadn't forgotten. I couldn't. He was a superstar now. And I was still catering parties for record execs who wouldn't give me the time of day professionally and fending off the wandering hands of Willie the pub owner and a dozen others like him at every gig the band and I scored.

Dex was the star of all my naughty fantasies and I constantly wondered if I had done the right thing, leaving him behind without even giving him my name.

The first time I met Dex Wilder I was wearing a toga and body glitter. The second time, it was handcuffs.

Chapter Two

Two Years Later

"I HATE Dex Wilder."

"No, you don't," Becca said, pouring the coffee. I took a sip, then peered back at the latest tabloid photos of him and another blond bimbo.

I didn't argue. We both knew she was right. "Look. Her boobs practically have their own ZIP code."

Becca peered across our tiny secondhand kitchen table and pulled the rag towards her. "Wow. Wonder what those cost?"

I snatched the tabloid back, balled it up and tossed it in the general direction of the garbage can. "It's disgusting."

"You're just jealous. You could have been the tour bunny of the hottest, richest, most popular country star since Johnny Cash, and you wouldn't even give the poor guy your phone number. Maybe it could have gone somewhere."

"Yeah, like the back of his tour bus. Besides, I don't want a boyfriend."

"So what's the problem?"

"The problem is, it's just not fair." I gestured to the tiny apartment just this side of shabby. "I mean, look at this place. I'm tired of playing to rednecks in seedy bars. Wondering if I'll serve enough crab cakes to make rent every month. Sending out demo tapes to every label in Nashville and getting absolutely nowhere."

I scooped the balled-up tabloid off the cracked linoleum. "And then there are people like Dex Wilder, who no sooner get to Nashville and sign a multimillion-dollar record deal to sing songs about his boots or his dog or how much fun it is to party all the time. Uggh!" I re-balled the tabloid and threw it in the can this time. And slammed the lid.

It didn't help that everywhere I looked, there he was. In the tabloids, magazine interviews, news shows, music videos, billboards, and of course the radio. God, those DJs loved Dex Wilder. Every time they played him, what popped into my mind? Hot, steamy, sex up against the wall of a public building. Which I hadn't experienced again since that night. If I had it to do over, I wouldn't change a thing. I just wished I could forget about him, the way he'd obviously forgotten about me.

I was determined to put Dex Wilder and the Bimbo of the Week out of my mind. I'd made the decision that night to make it a one-night stand and it was the right one. Dex was free to carry on with whomever he wanted.

I flipped to the review section of the *Sunday Tennessean*. My band, Road Kill, had played a gig the previous night at yet another stinky hole-in-the-wall, but I'd seen the music reporter pop in for a few minutes and hoped he'd have something nice to say about us, for a change.

He didn't.

"Road Kill lives up to its name again with second-rate covers and a few lukewarm originals. The only good thing about Road Kill is its lead singer, a Heidi Klum look-alike with a so-so voice. If Miss Stratton had shown a little more skin, patrons might have stayed for the second set."

I wadded up that paper, too. "Can you believe that jerk?"

"Well, you really should dress sexier on stage. Boobs are as important as voice, you know."

"That's ridiculous. Just because I happen to be blond and tall and well endowed, people think that's all there is. I don't want people to look at my boobs. I want them to hear my music."

Becca shrugged. "Your funeral."

I sat down again, the wind knocked from my sails. "It's not that I'm really jealous of Dex Wilder or anyone else who has made it. I'm just...tired. I never thought this would be so hard. Every time we take one step forward and it looks like something might finally go our way, something falls through and we're right back to square one."

I rubbed my eyes, still burning from playing the smoky bar the previous night. "This isn't working."

Becca got up and put her cereal bowl in the sink. "You need to do something drastic."

I raised my head and looked at her. "Like what? Go into Wildcat Records with a gun and force some record executive to listen to my demo?"

Rebecca smiled thoughtfully. "Well, that's definitely plan B, but I was thinking of something that carries slightly less jail time."

I'd tried it the right way, been the good girl, willing to pay her dues and do the work it would take to get that first contract with a big label. Yet here I was, two years later, still living hand to mouth, still playing crappy bars, still waiting tables for record company parties I'd never be a guest at.

It sucked.

All I'd ever wanted growing up in Indiana was to move to Nashville and make music. It was time to break out of the box and do something different. Big stars broke the rules. Big stars made things happen. Maybe it was time to take a risk.

"What kind of drastic move did you have in mind?"

* * * *

As I smiled and nodded at the last security guard standing between me and the performers' dressing rooms, I asked myself for the hundredth time how the heck I had let Becca talk me into sneaking into Sara Ann Reynold's dressing room to slip her my demo tape in person. Sara Ann was a huge star and had just been inducted into the Country Music Hall of Fame. Might as well aim high, right? She and a handful of other country stars were playing a charity concert and there were a lot of people milling around. It was the perfect opportunity for "drastic."

Becca's friend at the Sommet Center had assured us they let attractive, scantily-clad blondes backstage all the time without proper passes. So here I was in a borrowed dress that showed more cleavage than an overweight plumber's jeans, and heading into the shadowy backstage corridors to pimp my demo.

I finally made it into the hallway where the dressing rooms were located and started reading doors. There were rooms for the bands, rooms for refreshments, rooms for press, rooms for the stars. I kept reminding myself that Dierks Bentley had gotten his big break by slipping Brad Paisley his tape one night at the Opry. That seemed to have turned out well for Dierks and I was hoping for the same result.

"Hey," I heard a voice echo down the corridor. The silhouette of a large security guard who liked his doughnuts just a little too much was visible against the light from the main area. "Miss? I need to see your credentials."

Great. A rent-a-cop who was actually doing his job. Just what I needed. I glanced at the wall of doors. The security guard was far away and the lighting was dim at best. If I ducked into one of the dressing rooms, it would be hard for him to tell where I'd gone.

Then I could sneak back out after he was gone and locate Sara Ann's dressing room.

I turned the first knob on my right and slipped inside.

It was dark, which was good. That meant no one was home right now. Or maybe this particular room wasn't being used at all. Even better.

I flipped the lock on the door and pressed my ear to the door. After a minute, I heard the huffing and quick shuffling footsteps of the security guard and held my breath. I clutched the tape in my sweaty palm and prayed the guard had the IQ of a caterpillar.

I heard him opening doors further up the corridor, then closing them before moving on to the next. Shit. Why couldn't this guard go back to swilling beer and ogling groupies like the rest of his cohorts?

The guard was coming closer. His shuffling footsteps and jangling keys reminded me of all the horror movies I'd ever watched through fingers half-covering my eyes. Only this was for real, and though I might not be hacked to pieces with a chainsaw, being put in jail and having to call home for bail money would be almost as bad.

The doorknob wiggled and I heard the key in the lock.

I hid behind the door. With any luck, the guard hadn't seen me going into the dressing room. But I had never had good luck and when the doorknob turned, I sucked in my breath and held it, willing myself to go invisible.

"Miss?" the guard asked, flipping on the light. There was no point in hiding now. But maybe he could be persuaded to let me go without too much trouble.

I stepped out and smiled at him. "Hi."

He didn't smile back.

"What are you doing in Mr. Wilder's dressing room?"

Mr. Wilder. Shit. Not – "Dex?" I said in a groan.

"Yeah," he eyed my skimpy dress and gold heels. "Are you a *guest* of Mr. Wilder's?"

"Guest?"

He arched a brow.

"Oh, a guest," I said, feeling my cheeks burn. He thought I was a groupie. "No. Definitely not." Not on purpose, anyway.

He took a pair of handcuffs off his belt and approached me. "I'm afraid I'm going to have to take you in, then."

"What? For trespassing?"

"Mr. Wilder has gotten threats from women like you before. I'm head of his personal security team and we don't take chances."

I suddenly remembered reading about Dex being attacked in his dressing room in Tulsa by a crazed fan convinced she was his wife and he was her cheating husband. She'd had a gun and though it hadn't turned out to be loaded, well, I could see why he took pre-cautions now. Though I wasn't sure how I felt about being put in the same group as a woman currently incarcerated in a mental institution.

I backed away, deeper into the room, but the beefy guard fol-lowed me.

"Just calm down, now, ma'am, and we'll get this all straightened out, okay?"

"I'm not a stalker."

"Okay. We'll sort this all out. Just calm down."

He lunged then. He was much faster than he looked and before I knew it, I was on my belly and handcuffed just like one of those perps on *Cops*.

The guard hauled me to my feet. "Sorry, ma'am. But I'm going to have to run you in."

"Really," I said as he walked me towards the door. "I'm not a stalker. I don't even like Dex Wilder. I hate him!"

The door opened just as the last words left my mouth and stand-ing there framed in the doorway was the man himself.

"What the –" Shock was replaced by surprise, which was re-placed by a glare.

"I'm sorry, Mr. Wilder. I only left for a second to use the john and she slipped in. It's all taken care of now, though."

He tugged me forward, but Dex put a hand on the guard's arm.

"It's okay, Joe."

"You know her?"

He looked right into my eyes and every second of the night we shared two years earlier came rushing back.

"Yeah. I know her."

The guard jangled his keys and moved to take the cuffs off.

"Leave them," Dex said, still staring into my eyes, the naughty glint in full force.

"Sir?"

"And leave the key."

The confused guard shook his head a little and handed Dex the key before scurrying out of the room. Dex locked it behind him and turned to face me.

I swallowed hard.

"I can explain," I began, not at all sure I really could.

"Really." He circled me slowly, like a predator, and I was a little afraid. My knees felt weak and not in the same way they were the last time I'd seen Dex up close and personal.

"Yeah," I said. "I was looking for a different dressing room and came here by mistake."

He looked at my outfit up and down and I know I must have flushed head to toe under his stare.

"Well, you found mine."

He moved in closer until I was staring at the buttons on his shirt. He tiled my head up with one finger beneath my chin and forced me to look at his face.

"Lucky me," he whispered, showing that sideways grin I remembered before bringing his lips to mine.

He put one hand to the back of my head and kissed me with the same confidence and skill that I had remembered way too often over the last two years. When he licked the seam of my lips, they opened and he swept inside to taste me, tease me with his tongue.

I couldn't help it. I kissed him back, rising on tiptoes to reach him better. He groaned at my response and wrapped the second arm around my waist, tugging me against his long hard body.

"You still taste good," he said against my lips. "Sweet. And spicy, too. Just like I remember."

I grunted and a little thrill that he remembered me shot through my body.

I was kissing Dex Wilder. The Dex Wilder on all the posters and the one I'd seen on stage a few times from the cheap seats. And also the Dex from that long-ago summer night who overwhelmed me with his passion and pure sexiness. I wondered if I was having another very vivid dream.

"Unlock me," I said, leaning into him.

"Not a chance." He nibbled my ear.

"What?"

"I'm not letting you get away this time until I'm good and ready to let you go."

I should have been outraged, but deep in the back recesses of my mind, just this sort of set-up was always one of my wildest fantasies. To be taken willingly, with no choice in the matter, by a man so sexy and alpha that I couldn't resist even if I'd wanted to. It wasn't PC and wasn't something I'd ever admit to in the light of day, but handcuffed and helpless and in the arms of the one man who was the star of my naughtiest fantasies, well, that was different.

I nodded my assent – not that he needed my go-ahead – and turned my face to kiss him again.

The cowboy hat was the first thing to hit the floor this time. His hair was damp and his skin salty from performing on stage. I loved his scent, his taste, and everything he was making me feel deep inside. Warmth spread through my body as I imagined all the things he might do to me, none of which I could control or deny him.

"I need a shower, baby."

I blinked for a moment. "Okay. I guess I'll…wait?"

He smiled that slow smile and ran his hands down my sides, brushing the curve of my breasts, down to my waist, further to the flare of my hips and down to the outside of my thighs.

"Oh, no, you'll be with me."

His hand started back up under my dress this time, shoving it up as he went, back over all my curves, but on my skin this time.

He shoved my dress up and up until he tugged the strapless, stretchy number over my head, then down my bound arms to drop to the floor.

I wasn't wearing a bra, only silky black panties that didn't leave much to the imagination. I was aching by then and he used his thumbs on my breasts gently, that naughty grin still in full force as he stared into my eyes.

"Are you feeling dirty, too?"

I wet my lips. "Yeah."

He unbuttoned a few buttons of his shirt, then grabbed the back yoke and pulled it off over his head. I caught my breath. He'd been working out. He'd been hot before, with his broad chest and flat belly, but now he was all hard muscle and six-pack abs. His biceps were bulkier, too, and his chest even broader. When I'd seen his shirtless picture in some of the tabloids, I'd wondered if they had somehow enhanced the pictures. They hadn't. It was all Dex.

He sat down on a low footstool and tugged off his cowboy boots and socks, then popped the button on his fly and eased his zipper down.

His boxer-briefs left little to the imagination. It still took my breath away. Warmth pooled low in my belly and I could hardly wait for him to touch me.

Dex brought that delicious body close to mine and traced a line between my breasts, down my abdomen to my navel, where he flicked the gold ring there.

"Didn't see this the last time."

"It's new."

He got to his knees then looked up at me, putting his hands on my hips. "I like."

He traced my navel with his tongue, flicking the ring with each circle. Then he moved lower to the line of my panties.

He hooked his thumbs under the string waistband and tugged them down to expose me fully to his gaze.

With my hands behind my back, I couldn't do anything to hide myself, or distract him or even help him. I was completely at his mercy and at the moment, I couldn't think of anywhere else I'd rather have been.

He slid my panties down my legs and I stepped out of them. I was totally nude except for my red heels.

"I like this, too," he said and tugged my hips until he could bury his mouth between my thighs.

My head dropped back and a low, ragged groan escaped me. He used his tongue to circle and tease and delve inside just a bit until I was so eager, it was almost embarrassing. But he only gripped my hips harder and pressed deeper until my head felt like it was going to float off my shoulders. I swayed on my feet. It was a good thing Dex had a good grip on my hips.

With a final kiss, he got to his feet and kissed me on the lips. I could taste my own essence: a little salty, musky, and combined with Dex's unique flavor, perfect.

"See how good you taste, baby? I could do that all night."

He ran a hand through my hair and kissed me deeply again until all I could see, hear, smell, and think about was Dex and what I wanted him to do to me.

"Please," I groaned when he moved to my neck. "Please, Dex."

"I love it when you say my name like that." He was smiling that smile again, ornery, lids half lowered. I'd seen magazine shoots in which he flashed the camera the same sexy look and should have been immune by now. But that grin in person was deadly.

He helped me removed my shoes, then walked me backwards to the bathroom, kissing me all the while. When I stumbled, he caught me and pressed his body fully against mine, from lips to thighs. It was obvious he was as eager as I was.

He let me go to open the glass shower door and started the water.

"Don't you think you should undo me first?"

He pulled out the key and I actually felt a tiny stab of disappointment that my fantasy was coming to an end. But it was too late to take it back now.

I didn't have to worry. He unlocked my hands, then brought them both to the front and re-cuffed me. "Not a chance." He set the key on the bathroom counter, then returned to the shower to test the temperature.

"I hope you like it hot."

I nodded and licked my lips.

"Get in."

I stepped into the glass shower cube. The hot water warmed my skin and drenched my hair. Before I knew what he had in mind, Dex shed his underwear and stepped into the shower behind me. He lifted me easily with one arm around my waist and looped the chain of my handcuffs around pipe leading to the showerhead before setting me back on me feet.

My breasts pressed against the cool glass and the shower spray hit the back of my head and rolled down my back in hot rivulets.

"Okay?" he asked in my ear.

Oh, God, I was ready to blow right then just from the sensation of heat on my back and cold on my front and being completely at the mercy of Dex Wilder.

But I just nodded. "Yeah, I'm good."

"I knew you would be," he said, then nipped my ear and ran his hands down my sides to my hips. He pressed against me, the skin wet and slick now. I arched back, wanting him to complete this totally crazy fantasy of mine. But he just laughed softly and moved away. "Not yet, baby. There's a lot of hot water and I plan to use it all."

I heard the pop of a bottle top and his hands were back on me after a moment, hot and wet and slick with soap that smelled like almonds and vanilla.

He pushed my hair to one side and massaged my neck and shoulders, in hard, deep circles that made the rest of my bones melt away.

"That's right, baby, just relax for me." He smoothed his hands lower over the small of my back and my sides, then up my front, catching my aching breasts in his hands on the way.

He squeezed gently, pinching, then rubbing in circles. His hands were hot and wet and glided over my wet skin like satin.

He leaned in and kissed the side of my neck, his hard chest warming my back. I wanted to turn so I could get a good look at him wet and naked. But he wouldn't allow it. Dex nibbled my neck and earlobe and it was hard to tell where his tongue ended and the hot water began.

His hands moved lower over my abdomen and he hugged me to him, moving his hips slightly as if we were dancing under the shower spray. He nudged my belly ring. "Sexy. You're so sexy. You don't know how often I've thought of you. How many times I've thought of my golden goddess and her sweet body around mine."

I wasn't sure I believed that, given how many photos of him with his arm slung around assorted blondes I'd seen in tabloids and other trashy magazines, but hey, it was a fantasy. Why ruin it with cold hard facts when the only hard fact I cared about was pressing into my backside?

When his hands brushed the apex of my thighs, I bit my lips against the jolt of pure sensation that licked my body.

He glided over my sex to the inside of my thigh, then moved his hands back up again, brushing, teasing me until I wanted to shout with frustration. I wanted his hands on me and some part of him in me. But I was trussed and unable to do anything about it.

He kissed the side of my neck, nipping lightly as his fingers at last slipped inside me, right where I wanted them.

"You're so hot and ready for me."

"I know," I breathed. I closed my eyes, letting pure sensation, not rational thought, rule my body for once.

"Please, Dex."

"Please what, baby?" He brought one hand to my sensitized nipple while he used his fingers on the other hand to thrust slowly in and out of my body.

He plucked at me gently and I cried out, wanting more.

"How about this?" He added another finger to his thrusts and the delicious sensation caused a new round of shudders to quake though my body.

"Yeah. Like that."

"You like that I'm in control?"

"Yes."

His hand moved up my chest to my throat. He urged my head backwards until it lay against his shoulder and continued his ministrations below.

I was so turned on now I could barely stand up. But I couldn't sink down either with my hands stretched over my head.

He caressed my throat, and I felt my pulse beat against his fingers.

The warm spray hit me in the face, giving me a sense of total immersion in Dex. My eyes were closed, which only made the sensations more intense.

"Are you ready for me?"

"God, yes."

"Good. Because I'm going to pop right now just watching your gorgeous body all hot and wet for me."

He removed his fingers and grasped my hip with one hand as he guided himself into my body with the other.

I shifted my pelvis to give him better access and he slid all the way home. My breath hitched when he was finally sunk to the root, his front snug against my back. Dex wrapped his arms around my torso, hugging me to him so that there was no space between our bodies.

My arms ached with the tension of being chained above my head but I welcomed the discomfort as just another sensation to add to the heady mix of heat and pressure and friction Dex had woven around us.

Then he began to move. Slowly at first, sliding out, then slamming home again in a long, clean slide.

In and out, with my breathy sighs, he loved my body.

"God. Just like I remember," he whispered in my ear. His voice was raspy and low, a whisper all but lost in the drenching downpour of the shower.

I thrust backwards, wanting him to go faster. No more teasing, no more words. Just sex. Raw, dirty sex.

He got the picture.

Dex grabbed my hips and thrust harder until his wet flesh slapped against my backside. He grunted with each deep stroke and I was pretty sure I did, too. I felt lightheaded from the heat of the water and the heat building inside me.

Pressure coiled tighter and tighter until it burst suddenly like a popped balloon. Tendrils of pleasure spiraled through my limbs, through my belly, through my breasts, through my sex and took my breath away.

"Baby," Dex said as he stiffened and pulled away.

I groaned. He felt so good. Every part of him, every place he touched me was on fire for him.

He hugged me to him, squeezing me tight for a minute before chuckling in my ear. "Yeah, I remember that, too."

I smiled. "Me, too."

"Your arms must be getting awfully tired by now."

"A little," I fibbed. They were *really* tired and sore. But happy, just like the rest of me.

He lifted me up enough to drag the chain between the cuffs off the shower head and I was finally able to put them down. I winced.

"There you go, babe. You all right?"

I turned and smiled up at him. I'm great."

"Yeah. You are." He leaned in and gave me a quick peck on the mouth. "Here. Let me get your back."

Dex soaped up his hands and washed my back. Then his hands slid down to my backside, then between my legs. I wasn't complaining.

Dex turned me then and soaped up my front.

He looked down at me, the glint in his eye telling me he wasn't done with me just yet. I wasn't complaining about that, either.

He soaped me carefully, washing between my legs, then getting down on his knees to do my thighs, my calves, and even my feet. He gave my toes a quick kiss and stood up. "Water's getting cold."

I hadn't even noticed, but the water temperature had definitely cooled. My own temperature was rising again.

Dex reached behind me to turn off the shower, then shook his hair until it stood out in a spiky mess.

He opened the shower door and stepped out, then grabbed my arm to help me out.

"Let me dry you off." He rubbed me all over with the towel, the rough texture abrading my skin in all the right places.

I shivered in the cool of the dressing room, goose flesh covering my skin.

"If I take these off, do you promise not to run away before I get your number this time? And maybe even your name?"

I nodded. "I promise."

He used the key to twist open the lock and removed the handcuffs.

I rubbed my wrists. They were a little red, a little raw.

Dex grabbed them and inspected them, frowning. "I'm sorry, babe," he said, pressing a kiss to each. "I didn't mean to hurt you."

"It was definitely worth it," I said, teeth chattering.

He smiled down at me, his lashes dark and spiky from the water. "Yeah." He grabbed a fluffy white robe and wrapped it around me. I pushed my arms in and snuggled into its warmth. "I'm glad you came tonight," he said. "Even if you didn't mean to."

"Me, too."

"Come here. Sit down. Tell me what you've been up to since your Greek goddess days."

Dex pulled on a pair of boxers and rubbed his hair with a towel. He was the same cowboy, only not. There was a veneer of sophistication clinging to him now that said he had been places and seen things he hadn't when I'd last met him. I kind of missed the redneck in him.

"Well," I said. "The usual. Wreaking havoc on Mount Olympus. Serving beer to a bunch of no-account cowboys and singing for my supper."

He sat down on the couch and patted the spot next to him.

God, he was handsome. He had slung the towel around his neck, but aside from the boxers, he was still nude. His hair was pitch black when it was wet and he had the shadow of a beard just starting to show.

And he was looking at me.

"Still singing at the Wagon Wheel?"

"I can't believe you remembered that."

He looked at me seriously. "I remember everything about that night."

The intensity of his words made me uncomfortable. I didn't know whether to believe him or whether it was a line. I decided it was a line. After all, I'd seen photographic proof that he had women in every city. He probably whispered sweet nothings to each of them, too. Made each feel like she was the only woman in the world.

"Yeah, right."

He cocked his head. "What? You don't believe me?"

I shook my head and smiled at him. "Come on. You're Dex Wilder. You have different blonde on your arm every time I see your picture. TMZ calls it Bimbo of the Week. There's a gallery."

"Don't believe everything you read." Dex got up and opened the mini fridge in the corner. He pulled out two Diet Cokes and handed me one.

"Thanks," I said, suddenly uncomfortable again. I felt like I offended him. But I would be a fool to believe he'd actually remembered me from two years ago and that I was anything special to him.

Dex sat back down, but I could tell my words were still bothering him. We drank our Cokes in silence.

"You think I really don't remember?" he said at last, breaking the tension between us.

"I'm sure you remember that night, but I feel like it could have been any woman you remember sharing it with."

"You're wrong. But it sure would be nice to have a name to put with it."

I smiled. "It's Sydney. Sydney Stratton."

He smiled. "Sydney. Yeah."

The knock at his dressing room door startled us both. "Dex? Don't forget the meet-and-greet in fifteen minutes."

"Crap," he said under his breath. "My manager. Got it, Bob," he said, louder, and the knocker went away.

He stood up and went to the rack of clothing against the wall. "I hate this stuff," he said, pulling out a black shirt and black pair of jeans.

"What? The meet-and-greets?"

"All that stuff. I just want to sing."

I shifted on the couch. "Some of us dream about being so popular that people want to meet us. And greet us."

"I know. And I am grateful for everything that's happened these past couple of years. I'd be lying if I said I'm not." He pulled on the shirt and buttoned it while still facing me.

He pulled on his jeans, then sat down on a footstool to put on his socks and boots.

I watched him get ready in silence, enjoying the pure masculinity of his movements. It really wasn't fair that a man could pull on a couple of pieces of clothing, run his hands through his hair and look sexy as hell. It would take a woman a good hour or more to be ready to face the world. But Dex was so handsome, he could be wearing a wooden barrel and make every woman within a fifty-mile radius hot. *And* set them trying to figure out how to get inside that barrel.

"This won't take long," he said, picking up his hat off the floor. He brushed off the lint and settled it low on his head and cocked just slightly to the side, in his trademark fashion. "Will you wait for me, Sydney? Maybe we can grab something to eat. If you don't have other plans."

Warmth spread through me. Dex Wilder wanted to spend time with me. Dinner. Hell, that was practically a date. A date with a star.

"I'll be here."

Dex winked at me and in an instant a familiar expression, the one I'd see on posters and in countless magazines, masked his features that only a moment before had shown irritation at the responsibilities being a star brought.

"Be right back, babe."

Dex opened the door to his dressing room and all hell broke loose. Camera flashes, shouts and a crowd of fans and press mobbed him. He pushed forward through the crowd and I heard his security people yelling for everyone to back off and let Dex through, that he'd be happy to sign autographs as soon as he was done with the meet-and-greet.

I settled back into the cushions and found the remote.

I switched on the TV to the local news. I felt languid and content after the shower, but I was excited about spending more time with Dex, too. The spark between us two years ago was still there. And it didn't feel completely sexual. I felt as though we connected on many levels.

The weather came on. Hot. Then sports. Win. Then I heard the perky little newscaster say something that brought me to the edge of the couch cushion.

"And Dex Wilder was in town tonight. But it seems he got a little more than he bargained for when he returned to his dressing room after the sold-out charity appearance."

Sydney watched in horror as a jiggly videotape showed her, hand-cuffed and being manhandled by security. The tape was bumpy and the sound inaudible. All she could see was herself being dragged around in the handcuffs, makeup smeared, lots of skin showing, then the dressing room door closing with her inside.

"You may remember the incident last fall involving an apparently overzealous fan who threatened Wilder at a Tulsa, Oklahoma, concert. There is no word tonight if the woman taken into custody was armed. Wilder's head of security said only that the situation was well in hand. Next, new information on the price hike the state is considering for fishing licenses."

I sat staring at the television in total shock. I was most definitely not armed. And not a groupie.

Or was I?

I mean, twice now I had hooked up with Dex for a little kinky sex. I mean, he hadn't even known my name until about five minutes ago. I'd sneaked into his dressing room. Holy crap. Maybe I was a groupie. No better than the assorted blondes in the tabloids.

I grabbed my wrinkled dress off the floor and pulled it on. I slipped on my shoes and combed my fingers through my wet hair.

If it hadn't been me handcuffed to Dex's shower, it would have been some other blonde. And I wasn't going to stick around long enough for all the paparazzi to get a good shot of me with Dex. I was not going to be TMZ's Bimbo of the Week.

I pressed my ear to the door. It appeared to be quiet outside, the mob having probably followed Dex to his meet-and-greet.

Good. That meant a clean getaway.

I opened the door and, after making sure the coast was clear, disappeared into the shadowy hallway, taking only the memory of a perfect fantasy with me.

Chapter Three

MORNING IS not a good time of day for anybody working the club scene. Or the catering scene, for that matter. These are nocturnal jobs, and nine-to-fivers can't possibly understand that yes, I'm still sleeping at eleven because I didn't make it home from work until three or four in the morning, not because I'm lazy or "sleeping in" or taking it easy.

Try telling this to my mother, who without fail calls me at eight a.m. every Tuesday, expecting me to me up and dressed, apartment spotless, laundry done, errands run and dinner planned by that hour. Sometimes I think she found some time portal in the 1950s and just transported here, because on her worst days she definitely puts June Cleaver to shame. Me? Not so much.

So when the phone rang at eight a.m. on the dot, I groaned and struggled to get myself upright. I knew if I didn't answer, she'd be filing a missing person's report with Metro PD. Again.

"Hi, Mom."

"You sound awful. Are you sick again?"

I cleared my throat and took a swig of tepid water from the glass on my nightstand. "No, Mom. We had a gig last night. My voice is a little raw."

"Oh, that's nice. Her tone was just this side of condescending. But she was trying. "Did you have a good time?"

I rolled my eyes. Even after all this time, she didn't get it. "Yeah, it was great. The owner wants us to come back next week."

"That's wonderful! How much does that pay?"

I lied.

"How nice. Maybe you'll be able to come home for a visit. Or longer. You know, May down at the Ladies Auxiliary told me just the other day that they're looking for models for the farm implement display at the state fairgrounds next month. You could put together a portfolio and maybe…."

"Mom. I'm not modeling anymore. Especially not at the farm implement show."

"You're just so pretty, Sydney. God made you beautiful for a reason. I hate to see you waste it."

I gritted my teeth. My mom had used her looks from the age of five to get whatever she wanted. Beauty contests paid her way through college, modeling jobs supported her and let her travel the world, catalog ads had snagged her a rich husband and the perfect home she'd always dreamed of.

That was all fine for her, and I was even proud of her for what she'd accomplished. But she couldn't possibly understand why I wanted to do something different with my life. Why I needed to prove that I was more than just a pretty face. Or a trophy prancing along on a rich guy's arm.

I didn't even try to explain again. "I know, Mom." I flopped back on my pillow and stared at the cracks in the ceiling while she regaled me with tales about all the local gossip and how my sister's second pregnancy was going just perfectly. That led to the other sore point.

"Have you met any nice young men?" she asked casually, but I knew this was a huge source of stress for her. Because without a man, a woman was nothing, of course.

I could have told her I wild monkey sex the previous week, naked and handcuffed to a guy's shower, after I'd been nearly been arrested for breaking and entering. But I didn't think that was quite what she meant by nice young man and I loved my mom, so I gave the standard answer. "Not since you asked me last week, Mom. I really don't have time to date." Which was true. I just left out the part about not being able to get the one-night stand with Dex – both of them actually – out of my head long enough to even look at anyone else. And that I didn't want a boyfriend, anyway.

"You know, Nancy White's son is living in Knoxville. He's an attorney. Maybe I could give Nancy your number and –"

"Thanks, Mom. Really. I'm just too busy right now."

Mom sighed, defeated. "Well, let me know if you change your mind."

"Yeah. Sure will."

"Oh! My cake for the Ladies Auxiliary just dinged. Got to go, dear. Be careful. I don't like that you girls live alone down there."

"I'll be careful. Tell Dad I said hi."

The line went dead and the grilling and guilt trip was over for another week. Sometimes I wondered if I could just tape my end of the conversation and play it back every time she called. I hung up the phone and pulled the pillow over my head.

I'd dreamed of Dex, and the images that still lingered in my head, along with my mother's phone call, were giving me a hell of a headache. I still couldn't believe what I'd done. Maybe I'd had some vague hope that hooking up with him a second time would somehow exorcise the demon. That the sex hadn't actually been as good as I had remembered. That he hadn't made my body sing and my head fly off to parts unknown.

I was wrong.

And now I was feeling worse than usual. That was twice now that I'd slipped up and fallen under his spell. Twice I'd given into the wild need he seemed to bring to life in me. Twice I'd had dirty sex with him like some star-struck groupie. It was becoming a habit, and it had to stop.

"Hey, did you see this?"

Becca came charging into my tiny bedroom waving the new *Nashville Scene*. "There's going to be a contest for singer-songwriters. The winner gets a development deal with Big Dream records."

I pulled the pillow off my head and sat up. "Really? Let me see that."

I scanned the page and read the notice. It looked legit.

"All you have to do is send in your demo tape," Beccca encouraged. "Then they'll narrow it down to twenty-five semi-finalists."

The demo tape. "Crap. I think I left my last one in Dex's dressing room." Along with my panties and my self-respect. I had a feeling I wasn't getting those back either.

"Uh-huh," Becca said, sitting on the side of my bed. "And how did that go?"

I re-read the contest notice. "I'm not a 900 number, Becca. You'll have to get your jollies somewhere else." Becca hadn't been home much recently. She had some new boyfriend and he had gotten her a gig singing demos for a group of songwriter friends he had.

She stood up. "You're no fun at all. Girls are supposed to share this stuff."

I looked up at her and grinned. She *had* pointed out the contest to me. "All I will say is that handcuffs were involved."

"Oh. My. God."

I smiled and turned my attention back to the contest ad.

"The entry deadline is coming up," I said. "I'll have to ask one of the guys if I can buy one of their tapes. Surely one of them has one lying around."

"You could call Dex and see if he can return the one you lost." She grinned. "And then maybe you two could...."

"Not a chance. There won't be a repeat performance."

"Why not? Don't tell me he's lost his touch."

"It's not that." It was that if I saw him a third time, I'd want there to be a fourth. And a fifth. And where could a relationship based solely on sex with the playboy of the country music world really go, even if I did want a relationship at all? Nowhere. That's where. And I didn't have the time or energy to chase a bad boy, or any boy, around. I now had a contest to win.

Becca shrugged. "I think you're crazy. Every female under the age of eighty would give her left tit for ten minutes alone with that guy. And you won't even give him your number." She shook her head. "Just think what he could do for your career. No more seedy bars and smoky clubs. I'll bet he could hook you up with his people."

"When I get hooked up with 'people,' I want it to be because of my voice and my music, not because I've slept my way into a record deal."

Becca tightened the belt on her robe. "Look. You've got talent. That's obvious. But so do half the newbies in Nashville. What's wrong with using your other charms to get a little attention?"

She had a point. "I don't know. I'm just not comfortable with it. It just seems so mercenary."

"It is. But that's business." Becca headed to the door of my bedroom. "Use the advantages you've got. Everyone else is."

Becca left and I lay back in bed, thinking. My mother would be thrilled beyond belief if I managed to snag some rich record executive and brought him home for Thanksgiving dinner. But what if he wasn't a record exec? What if he was a struggling musician just as broke as I was? Maybe from some small little Southern town with nothing but the dust on his boots.

A melody and a few tinkling lyrics began to bloom inside my head and I grabbed the notebook I always kept beside my bed.

I closed my eyes and let the silent music roll as I envisioned the set-up. A boy. From the wrong side of the tracks. A girl. In a big white house with the picket fence. He loves her, but he knows he's not good enough for her. Her family will object. He doesn't have anything to offer her but his heart. The image turned into a chorus and I scribbled it down before it was gone:

I know I'm no good for you

I know you're too good for me

I know we both know it's true

Baby, I know.

I closed my eyes and envisioned the guy. Not surprisingly, he looked like Dex. Or like Dex might have looked ten years ago. But I didn't fight it. I just let the words and the music come. I didn't have all the lyrics yet, but I scribbled down what was there:

I saw you at the (something rhyming with Mama)

Standin' by your Mama

Baby, you took the breath from me

You stopped me in my tracks, girl

Put me on my back, girl

Made a total fool outta me

(Chorus)

I grabbed a small tape recorder and sang what I had with the melody playing in my head. I would work it out better later on the piano or guitar, but I wanted to get the basic tune down before I forgot.

I sang it through a couple of times, making small changes, trying a few different variations in the tune as well. When I played back the recording, I smiled. It was a long way from a finished song, but it was a start. The thrill of creative energy flowing through my head was a kind of high, and I jumped out of bed and headed for the shower, still whistling my new tune.

Dex? Dex who? I was a force in my own right and didn't need his star power to make it in the business.

At least not today.

* * * *

"I think you need to sex it up a little more, Syd," said Bobby, Road Kill's bass guitarist.

"Yeah, maybe if you wear a real short skirt and get one of those bras that, you know," Ted held his hands up to his chest like he was cupping a pair of double Ds. "Boost 'em a little."

"I am not wearing a push-up bra just to get a bunch of drunk frat guys in here on Thursday nights," I said, wrapping up the mic wires. "And I'm not going to 'sex it up.' We want people who will come for the music, not come to look at my short skirts."

"Couldn't hurt," Dillon, the lead guitarist, said with a grin. Dillon was the sweet one of the bunch and I was pretty sure he had a crush on me.

I'd hooked up with Road Kill right after arriving in Nashville. They'd posted fliers around town looking for a lead singer. I had answered it. They, being guys, hired me before I could even sing a note for them. I made them sit though an audition anyway. They had been on the scene a little longer than me and had the contacts I didn't at the time. It had seemed like a good arrangement, but it really wasn't getting me where I wanted to go. I had considered leaving the group a few times, but as long as I was getting out there and booking shows, it seemed like a bad idea to just quit.

"Hey, do you guys have any of the demo tapes we made last year? There's a singer songwriter contest I want to enter and I…lost my last one before I could make copies."

"Sorry. Gave mine to a cute redhead last week to try to get her to go out with me," Bobby said, setting his guitar reverently in its case.

"Sorry, Syd. Sent all mine out," Dillon said, frowning.

"That's okay. Thanks anyway. Ted? Surely you've got one left." There was no way Ted had taken a break from partying long enough to do any actual work towards trying to get us a deal.

"I have whole box in the trunk of my car."

"Cool. Can I get one? I'll buy the first round." Beer was always a good form of currency with this group.

"I sold the car last week."

"With the tapes still in the trunk?"

He shrugged. "I was kind of hammered. Still. Sorry, Syd."

Great. I was working with idiots. And I still had no tape.

"Maybe you can get some studio time over at Big Fish and make a new one," Dillon suggested. "I heard they're pretty cheap."

I mentally calculated how much I had available on my Visa card. It might just work. It would be nice to have a new one, anyway, since the first one hadn't gotten me anywhere and I could record my new song.

"I'll check. Thanks, Dillon."

He smiled at me. "Any time."

"Hey guys, great set."

We all looked up at the same time. The bar had mostly cleared out. It was near closing time and last call had already gone out.

The man was on the short side, balding, and wore khakis with a button-down shirt. It was a label guy, or maybe an agent. Hope surged in my chest and I smiled at him.

His dark eyes narrowed on me and he smiled back. "You got a minute, doll?"

I glanced back at the guys. They were looking at each other and didn't appear too happy.

"Okay," I hesitated, not wanting to tick off the rest of the band. It could be nothing. Heck, it probably was nothing.

He reached a hand out to help me hop down from the stage and I took it. He didn't let go once I was on solid ground again, but rather led me to a table near the bar. He held out a chair for me and the way he looked at me made my skin crawl. Of course, if he was a record exec, that made sense.

He sat down across from me and smiled again, showing his too-white teeth. "Want a drink?"

"No," I said. "Thank you." I cocked my head. "What is this about?" I softened my question by smiling at him.

He sat back in his chair and looked at me with the confidence of a man who always got whatever he wanted. Just the attitude alone was a turn off, but I could deal with a lot if it meant Road Kill had gotten the attention of a producer or scout or whatever this guy was.

"I heard your set. You've got a great look." His gaze wandered from my face to my boobs. I crossed my arms over my chest and stopped smiling.

"And?"

"The voice is okay. The band is…mediocre. But I think I can help you."

"Oh, really?" I was getting a bad vibe from this guy already.

He leaned forward and brushed a tendril of hair behind my ear. I cringed and wanted to pull away, but I forced myself to stay still, staring at him. "Who are you, exactly?"

"Ron Lennart. With Milton Records."

That was supposed to impress me, apparently.

"What kind of help did you have in mind?" I asked, though I already knew the answer. The guy was a toad and it wasn't the first time I'd been propositioned.

"I thought maybe some voice lessons, maybe some time in the studio. Who knows, I might even be able to get your demo in front of Mr. Milton himself."

Milton was famous for taking nobodies and making them into somebodies. But I wasn't going to pimp myself out for a tape. Especially when it meant alienating the rest of my band.

I pulled back, away from his slimy touch, and stood up.

"I'm not going to sleep my way to the top for a record deal," I said loud enough for the bartender and a few waitresses left cleaning up to hear. "And if that's the only way you can get a woman in bed" – I looked down my nose at him and narrowed my eyes – "that's just sad."

I heard the waitresses snicker and Ron's face turned bright red. His bald head shone with sweat as he glared back at me.

"Stupid slut," he hissed. "You don't know who you're dealing with." He shoved back from the table, knocking his chair over, and strode calmly out of the bar as if he was too good for it. For any of us.

Dillon rushed over. "Are you okay, Sydney?" Concern furrowed his brow. He really was a handsome, kind guy and had more talent than our other two bandmates combined.

"I'm fine. Just another jerk looking for an easy piece." I smiled at Dillon to let him know I was fine. "Occupational hazard."

"'Cause I could go after him, if you want."

"No, I'm fine. It's not worth your time. Come on, let's finish packing up. I'm really tired."

When all the equipment was packed up and stowed in the back of Bobby's van, I flipped open my cell phone and checked the messages. I always left my phone on vibrate in my pocket during the show because in the places we played, you never knew when a bar fight was going to break out and a call to 911 would become necessary.

There was one new message, but I didn't recognize the number. If it was that lawyer from Knoxville my mom was trying to hook me up with, so help me, I was going to kill someone.

It wasn't the lawyer.

"Hey Sydney. It's Dex Wilder. You left before I got back the other night and I just wanted to let you know I…had a great time."

I could hear the smile in his voice and the party in the background. Had he called me from a show or was it from his infamous party bus? Feminine squeals punctuated the general noise.

Party bus, definitely. Probably full of bimbos and Budweiser. It was surprising he gave me a thought at all, let alone bothered to call.

"I wish you would have hung around a little longer."

His voice had gone husky and, if I closed my eyes, I could imagine he was right next to me, whispering all the things he would have done to me had I stayed. It wasn't fair for a guy with a voice as rich and deep and sexy as his to use it for such nefarious purposes. It was like a secret weapon that found its mark every time.

"I found your tape, too, and gave it a listen. Not bad. So. Call me sometime, Sydney. You've got the number."

The message ended and I snapped my phone closed.

"Anybody I know?" Bobby asked, closing the doors to his beat-up van we used to carry our stuff.

"No," I said. Which was true. I was sure none of them was hanging out at Dex's house on the weekends. They would all flip a lid if they knew Dex Wilder had just called my cell phone, and they'd ask a bunch of questions I just didn't want to answer. "Just a guy."

"Uh-huh. Holding out on us, huh?" Ted asked with a grin. "Thought you wasn't into the whole dating thing."

"I'm not. It's just a friend. I don't even know how he got this number."

"Right. None of my 'friends' makes me turn red as a tomato when they call," Bobby said. "Hey, that reminds me, what's Becca doing these days?"

All the guys grinned then, and I suspected they all had a little bit of a thing for her. She came to our shows sometimes and always "sexed it up."

"She's busy," I said. "And she has a new boyfriend."

"Crap," Ted grumbled. "Missed my chance again."

I smiled. "Gotta be quick with that one."

"Oh, I can be quick."

"Yeah that's what Sarah Jean said," Bobby teased, ribbing his brother. "Quick."

"Shut up, man." Ted pushed Bobby on the shoulder. Bobby pushed back and a semi-playful wrestling match broke out.

"You ever get the feeling we're dealing with children here?" Dillon asked.

"Yeah. Daily."

"It wasn't that jerk who was just in here, was it?"

I thought of Dex's deep sexy voice saying my name and felt myself blushing all over again. "No."

Dillon gave me a small smile. "Well, whoever he is, he's a lucky guy."

Chapter Four

I SLAMMED the phone down and marked the name of another studio off my list. "Well, it's official. I'm screwed."

Becca stopped applying her third coat of mascara and looked at me. "Really? Two Toad was booked, too? That place is a dump."

I stood up and got a glass of water from the tap. "Apparently this contest is big news and everybody and their brother has booked studio time to get a tape together. Nobody has any space until after the contest deadline. Nobody I can afford, anyway."

"That sucks."

"Yeah." I picked up the contest flier and frowned at it. It was no wonder everyone in town was so jazzed about this thing. Half the battle was getting your stuff past the administrative assistants and into the tape players of someone who could actually do something if they liked your music. Getting to the semi-finals guaranteed you'd at least be heard by someone looking for talent. And if you made it to the top ten, there was a television special, a sort of on-air talent contest. Even the losers of that gig would come out winners. The exposure was gold, and just standing out from the crowd of other country music hopefuls was a boon.

Of course, not having a demo to submit to the open call wasn't going to get me anywhere.

"The guys don't have the old ones?"

"Already checked," I said, wadding up my list and tossing it in the garbage. The flier I put on the beat-up old fridge with the guitar-shaped magnet I'd bought at the first gas station I'd stopped at when I crossed the Tennessee border. I thought it would be my good luck charm. What an idiot.

Becca put down the makeup. "You could call Dex Wilder."

"No. Absolutely not."

"Why?" She came out of the bathroom and put a tube of lipstick in her purse. "He called you first. And he *has* your tape. Maybe he'll mail it to you." She grinned. "Or maybe he's got a studio in his house. He could give you a little one-on-one time."

I gave her the look. "No way." Even though it was an idea I had briefly entertained, I had banished it almost immediately. I knew Dex would probably help me out. And it wasn't that I thought he'd be another Ron Lennart, wanting to trade studio time for bedroom time. It wasn't Dex I didn't trust. It was me.

Plus, I hadn't returned his message from the other night. What did you say to a guy you'd let chain you to his shower and do all sorts of delicious things to you, then skip out on when he turns his back? Emily Post didn't cover that situation. I'd looked.

"I can't call him."

Becca shrugged. "If you want a shot at the recording contract, I don't think you have another option."

I crossed my arms over my chest. "I hate it when you're right."

She blew me a kiss and a wink before heading to the door. She had a date and, from the care she'd taken in getting ready and the handful of condoms she'd stuffed into her purse, I knew I wouldn't see her before morning.

The apartment was relatively quiet for a Thursday night, and it was a rare occasion when I didn't have to work or sing. I flipped through our basic cable stations but nothing caught my attention.

I got up and wandered to the fridge, but nothing caught my attention there, either. I considered working on my song, but my mind had not stopped turning over the problem with the demo and I had a feeling my muse wouldn't come out to play tonight. I didn't see a way to get myself into the contest. Not without a tape.

I grabbed a Diet Coke from the fridge and went to my bedroom. I'd listen to some music, get my mind off certain problems and certain people, and maybe the muse would make an appearance. Road Kill and I usually covered well-known stuff, but they let me work in a few of my own songs every now and then. Dillon wrote with me sometimes, working out the guitar parts while I was on the piano, the lyric-and-melody half of the writing team.

I turned on the radio and lay on my bed, closing my eyes. I listened idly for a while, just drifting, trying to relax, maybe even on the verge of sleep, when an idea struck me.

It was that first taste of passion, of connection, of chemistry. A passionate encounter that took two people by surprise with its strength, its unexpectedness. I pictured Dex, kicking out that spotlight. I thought about how good his hands had felt on my body. How his kiss had been like a lifeline to me at that moment, so caught up in the moment.

A new melody began to stream through my head. Harder. High energy. Driving. I sat up, switched off the radio and grabbed my notebook to write down what I heard in my head.

I liked the harder edge to the chorus that kept running through my mind as well as the softer parts in between. It had a driving bass, the kind you feel in the pit of your stomach. The kind that mimics the act the song describes. I liked the long looks, the sensuality of it. An hour passed, then two, and I was still scribbling, still hearing music in the silence of my bedroom. It was sexy and sweet, too. Sort of a look back, but also right in the moment.

The problem was the ending. A song was like a story, and I didn't yet know how my story ended. What happened when that hot glow was over? Did my lovers part ways and only know each other in memories from that point forward? Or did that one-night stand turn into more? I didn't know. I just didn't know.

Images of Dex nude and smiling over at me invaded my scattered thoughts. I was getting warm just thinking about how hot he'd made me. How just hearing his voice on the message I hadn't returned had made my gut clench and my body flush. His scent was still vivid in my mind. So were his taste and the way he'd held my head when he kissed me.

The jingle of my cell jolted me out of me thoughts. Flustered, I grabbed for the phone and answered it before I looked at the Caller ID. "Hello?"

"What are you wearing?"

My eyes flew open. I recognized the deep, rich voice immediately, of course. I'd just been fantasizing about it. "Dex."

He laughed. "Was it that obvious?"

I smiled, too. "Yeah. It was. I don't get many obscene phone calls these days."

"I guess I'll have to call more often, then."

I didn't know how to answer. I knew he was a big-time flirt and could very well have had a blonde on his lap right now.

I decided to keep it light. "So what are *you* wearing?"

"Right now?"

"Yeah." I rolled to my side and closed my eyes.

"Sweatpants."

"Oooh. Sexy."

He laughed. "I just got out of the shower."

Now there was an image. Tingles raced up my spine and I knew he was remembering a certain shower we'd shared. "Did you have a show tonight?" I asked.

I heard ice clink and what sounded like soda filling a glass. "Yeah. Houston. We're getting ready to head back East. We have a stop in Memphis tomorrow night, then we're home for a few days."

"Well, it must not have been much of a show."

"Why?"

"I don't hear a party this time in the background. Unless it's just a party for two tonight."

I bit my lip. I didn't want to sound like I cared about what he did. It wasn't as if we were anything more than a couple of people who had hooked up a couple of times.

I could hear the smile in his voice. "No, I'm flying solo tonight. You?"

"Nobody home but me and the cockroaches."

"Damn, wish I was there."

This was so awkward, like high school all over again, only without the zits.

"Why?" I sounded a little too breathy, even to my own ears.

"I think you know." His voice was huskier now, an octave deeper. It sounded as if he was right there with me. Heat stirred low in my belly.

"Oh yeah?" I couldn't resist. Working on that song about sex and passion and heat, well, it had gotten me a little hot.

"Yeah." I heard the ice clink again and him swallow. "Are you sitting or standing?"

I knew where this was leading. I knew it was a bad idea. I just couldn't remember why.

"I'm lying down on my bed."

He groaned. "You're killing me. Are you naked?"

"Not yet." I rolled to my back and popped the button on my fly. "I'm unzipping my jeans."

"Take them off."

I pushed the denim over my hips and kicked them to the floor.

"What do your panties look like?"

It was laundry day. I was wearing a pair of ratty old cotton granny panties. "Satin. Black g-string."

He grunted low in his throat. "Take off your top."

I set the phone down and turned off the bedside light before tugging my tank top off over my head. I put the phone back to my ear. "It's off."

"I'm on my bed now, too. It's dark and all I can hear is the hum of the bus's engine and your voice."

I closed my eyes. "Why don't you take off your sweatpants?" I said in a slow, deep whisper.

"Okay." There was a soft shuffling sound and my pulse went up a notch, just imagining him clean and damp from his shower, lying there in the dark in the middle of his bed wearing nothing but a pair of clinging boxer-briefs.

"Okay. I'm naked."

"No underwear?" I amended my mental image and my pulse went up another notch.

"Nope." I could hear the smile in his voice and warmth rushed straight to the pit of my stomach.

"Your turn," he said. "Take off your bra."

I smiled this time. "Not wearing one."

He groaned. "Panties, then. Take off your panties, Sydney."

My name on his lips sent a rush of heat straight to my sex. I was already lifting my hips to slide the granny panties over my hips and off.

"Okay. They're off." I rubbed a hand over my torso, my skin already heating, wondering how far he would take this.

I should have known by now that Dex was not the kind of guy to do anything halfway. It was all the way or nothing. And tonight, I was fine with that.

"God, Sydney. I can just imagine you lying there, all that gorgeous blond hair spread out over your pillow."

I tugged out the band that had held my hair back into a messy ponytail and spread it out, just as Dex had described.

"Yeah," I said softly.

"Touch yourself, Syd. Touch those gorgeous breasts for me."

My hand went to my breast and I cupped it briefly before moving my fingers over my nipples. I shuddered at the easy pleasure of it.

"Are you doing it?"

"Yeah," I breathed.

"Tell me what it feels like."

"I feel tingly all over. Especially when I pinch myself a little."

"I want to put my mouth on you. I want to taste you."

"Me too."

I was getting hot. My hips moved of their own volition and the sheet was getting all bunched up. My skin burned where my hand teased my breast and in the dark, I could hear every intake of Dex's breath. Every movement he made came through clear as a bell.

I pictured him lying there on his bed. "Now you," I said, still massaging my breast. "Touch yourself."

"Where?"

"Run your hand down your chest. Slowly." I took a shaky breath. "Now down over your abs and lower."

"God. Sydney." He groaned and I knew he was touching himself.

"Now stroke yourself. Slowly."

I licked my lips, wishing my hands were on his body.

"I'm so ready for you, baby." His breath whistled through his teeth and I squirmed, imaging him pleasuring himself, thinking of me.

"You. You, too." He gasped. "Touch yourself."

I didn't need to be told twice. I slid my hands over my soft belly to the place that hummed with desire.

"Feel good?"

"Oh yeah," I said, my fingertips gliding over hot flesh. "Really good."

"Oh, God. Put your fingers inside."

I slipped two into my opening and couldn't stifle the groan.

"That's right, baby. In and out." He was out of breath and I imagined him stroking himself faster and faster, his movements matching mine.

I bit my lip and squeezed my eyes shut. Pressure built inside me and I squeezed my legs together. Usually this wasn't enough to do it for me, but here in the darkness, with Dex's voice in my ear, knowing he was touching himself at the same time my fingers were inside me – well, it was more than enough.

"Feel good, baby?"

"Yeah."

"Faster now."

I squeezed my eyes shut as pressure built and built inside me. I wedged the phone between my shoulder and my ear and used my other hand to rub my ache. Pleasure spiked through me.

"I'm…using both hands, now. God. It feels so good."

"I know, baby." He was almost panting now.

"I'm so hot for you, Dex…I don't think I can –"

"I'm right with you, baby. Come on, Come with me."

My nipples tingled, my skin burned. Blood pumped through my body fast enough to make me dizzy. The friction of my fingers, the pressure on my sweet spot, the heat, the wetness, the sound of Dex pleasuring himself right in my ear, it all coalesced in an instant in a blinding flash.

I cried as the pleasure overtook me in hot waves and wanted to sob with the pure sensation of it.

I heard Dex's deep groan and gasp, too. Thinking of him nude, his hard abs contracting in pleasure sent another twinge reverberating though my sweaty body.

"Are you okay?" I asked after a moment.

"Yeah. You?" He was still panting.

"That was…I've never done that before."

"Never pleasured yourself?"

"No. I mean, yes, but not…over the phone."

"Me neither."

I brushed a sweaty tendril of hair off my forehead and sat up.

"Really?" It gave more sort of a perverse thrill to know that he wasn't burning up the lines every night of the week talking dirty to a different girl. It made me feel a little less like a groupie.

"Nope. Never."

"Huh."

"I think I'm going to need another shower. I'm a sweaty mess again, thanks to you."

Yum. "You started it," I said playfully.

"Yeah. I did." He didn't sound the least bit sorry. I wasn't either. "But that's not why I called."

I swung my legs to the side of the bed and turned on the light. "Why did you call?"

There was a long pause. "I just wanted to talk to you." Another pause. "You left pretty suddenly the other night. I thought we were going to grab some dinner."

"Well, I...remembered something I had to do," I said. It sounded like a lie, even to my ears.

"Okay," he said after a minute. "Fair enough."

I cleared my throat. "I'm glad you called, too."

"You are?" The smile was back in his voice.

"Yeah. I left my tape in your dressing room, and I kind of need it back."

"Oh." Was that disappointment?

"There's this contest I want to enter and that was my last copy."

I heard him take a drink. "Did you write those songs on the tape?"

"Yes." I fidgeted. It was hard sharing your stuff with someone whose opinion you cared about. "Mostly."

"They're good, Sydney. Really good."

My chest fluttered at his praise. My cheeks burned and I'm sure I was blushing. "Thank you."

"Tell you what. I'll give you back your tape if you'll have dinner with me at my house on Saturday night."

A little thrill of anticipation shot through me. "At your house?"

"Yeah." He paused and I could tell he was uncomfortable. "Sometimes it's hard to go out. Especially if you really want to talk to the person you're eating with. Get to know them better."

I swallowed. This was dangerous territory and I was slipping fast. "What if I say no to dinner?"

"I'll still give you the tape." He paused. "But I'd really like to see you again, Sydney. Show you my place."

"Okay," I said before I could overthink things. "What time do you want me there?"

"Eight." I heard Dex's smile again. "And wear that black g-string."

Chapter Five

BEYOND THE major interstates and the city blocks surrounding my apartment, I was hopelessly lost when it came to navigating Nashville. So many freeways crisscrossed, ran on top of each other and had signage that made no earthly sense that it usually rendered Internet-produced directions useless. I had literally thrown them out the window on a couple of frustrating occasions. So after spending way too much time picking out a little black dress, doing my hair and applying makeup, I left my apartment plenty early for the dinner date at Dex's house.

Dex lived south of Nashville in an area where many wealthy music industry people lived, and passing all the mansions and gated communities and fancy shopping malls with store names I only saw on *Sex and the City*, I was feeling completely nervous and totally out of my element.

What the hell was I doing? A hookup – okay, two – and a little phone sex was one thing. Going to his house for dinner, that was something else. A moment of weakness after an amazing phone-sex climax, maybe. Sure, I needed that demo tape back, but if I was honest with myself, I wanted to see him, too. Sex with him was becoming like a drug. The more I had, the more I wanted, even though I knew it was a very bad idea. I wasn't a good-time girl and that was the only place I could see this thing going.

Google directions didn't fail me for once and I headed west out of Brentwood. I passed multimillion-dollar gated homes, beautiful mansions set high on hilltops, peeking through trees, and long, winding driveways with intricate landscaping that probably cost more in upkeep than I made in a year.

I eventually found myself on a tiny two-lane highway. On one side of the road, trees and thick forest crowded the asphalt. On the other were open green fields that rolled to the horizon, just as I remembered from back home. Black cows dotted the span of green and the sun dipped low in the sky, casting a golden glow over everything.

No wonder Dex liked it out here. It was quiet and open and you felt like you could breathe. I began to relax a little. I kept driving, passing farmhouses and barns and more livestock and was just beginning to think Google had led me astray again when I came to a long, wrought-iron fence. I slowed down. I had to be getting close.

When I got to the gate, I saw the street number on a small black plaque and my heart did a quick flip-flop. I was here.

There was an intercom box but the gate was open, so I drove slowly down the winding gravel driveway, squinting against the gathering darkness to see his property.

The driveway angled up and as I climbed the small hill, the trees got thicker and thicker until I felt like I was Little Red Riding Hood going to meet a wolf deep in an enchanted forest. It got darker, the trees blocking out what was left of the sunlight. I leaned forward in my seat, wondering if there really was a house back here. Then I rounded the final curve and the house came into view.

I stopped the car.

Damn. Country music sure paid well.

Constructed of wood, stone and glass, Dex's house was like log cabin castle. It was two stories high, with sort of an octagonal tower in the middle and two wings jutting out at forty-five-degree angles on each side. Light blazed from walls made almost entirely from glass on the left side, while the right side, which I guessed was probably bedrooms, was dark.

I pulled through the circular drive to the front of the house, not really knowing where to park. Flipping the visor down to check my hair, I took a deep breath and told myself again that this was just dinner. No biggie. I grabbed my purse off the passenger seat but before I could reach for the handle, the driver's side door opened and there stood Dex, smiling down at me.

"You're here."

He said it as if he wasn't sure I'd show. Hell, even I wasn't sure I'd have the nerve.

"Yeah. Only about three U-turns this trip."

He took my hand and helped me out of the car. "I should have offered to pick you up."

"No, it's fine," I said thinking of my shabby little apartment. "I made it." I pulled my skirt down a little and tucked a tendril of hair behind my ear.

"You look beautiful."

I should. I'd spent way more than I could afford on a new outfit. It was no designer gown, but the shortish skirt and V-neck top set off my blond hair and hugged my trim figure. Okay, so I'd sexed it up a little. The band boys would be proud.

"Thanks. So do you."

Dex wore black pants and a light blue button-down shirt, open at the collar. He wasn't wearing the hat, but a pair of shiny black boots were on his feet. His hair was a little damp at the ends and he smelled like he'd just showered. He'd shaved and there was no trace of that shadow beard he'd practically trademarked. He looked younger and almost innocent.

Almost. I liked this version of Dex. And that was a dangerous thing.

"Come on in."

He led me inside, never letting go of my hand, and I knew I was about to be wined and dined and God knew what else. But for now, Dex was on his best behavior.

The interior of the house was even more spectacular than the outside. It was almost like being in a grown-up's version of a tree house. All around us, natural materials made it feel like were still outside. The transition from outside to inside was nearly seamless. Everywhere I looked, it was stone or wood or glass.

The floor in the entry was gray limestone, and heavy dark wood accents in the tall, narrow door frames and the rustic table and chair gave it almost a medieval castle feel. That opened up into a great room that took my breath away.

The cathedral ceilings and stone fireplaces, furniture upholstered in red-brown leather, Native American print rugs on the wood and stone floors all provided a feeling of casual, welcoming warmth. The floor-to-ceiling windows revealed the setting sun through the grove of trees on top of Dex's own little mountain and the room was flooded with soft, natural lighting. I felt a little like I had stepped into the pages of *Architectural Digest*. But in a strange way, it felt homey and comfortable.

"So this is the living room," Dex said, finally dropping my hand.

I looked around and nodded. "It's gorgeous. You do the decorating yourself?"

He chuckled. "No. It came decorated, actually. The guy who had the house built only lived here a short time. All the furnishings stayed." Dex walked deeper into the room and I followed. "My only addition was a sixty-five-inch flat-screen and a sound system."

He picked up a remote off the top of an armoire and hit a button. A soft jazzy tune filled the room, echoing off all the stone and wood so that it felt like there was a live band right there in the room with us. "You gotta have a good stereo."

I smiled. "Of course. What's upstairs?" I nodded towards a curving iron staircase set against the wall near the entryway.

"Come on. I'll show you." There was a glint in his eyes as he approached me. The innuendo was clear and fluttery warmth shot though my abdomen. God, he was dangerous.

"Okay."

He smiled and led the way up the stairs. At the top, there was a railing that overlooked the living area we'd just left and a hallway. We went down the hallway, passing several closed doors before Dex opened one near the end of the room and went inside.

"This is where I spend most of my time when I'm not on the road."

I was expecting a huge, decadently appointed bed. Maybe a brass headboard. A sex swing hanging from the exposed rafters in one corner. Assorted kinky items. Or maybe a collection of groupie underwear nailed to the ceiling like a frat-house wall of fame. Instead I found about a half-dozen guitars on stands, a computer desk and PC, a comfortable-looking sofa, a coffee table filled with tapes and all along one whole wall, built-in shelves packed to overflowing with CDs and DVDs and books.

"This is my library."

I walked over to his CD collection. "Wow. You have a lot of music."

"You should see my iPod. Best invention ever."

I perused the titles. You could tell a lot about a person by what music he listened to and what books were on his shelf. If this eclectic mix was any indication, Dex was a very complex individual. He had everything from big band to The Who to '80s hair bands, and basically the entire history of country music, from Patsy Cline to Taylor Swift, all on one wall.

And the books. He had a lot of books on history, and an equal amount of fiction and biographies, mostly of musicians and presidents. Scattered among all the volumes were framed pictures, many of kids.

"Who are they?"

"Nieces and nephews, mostly. That's my sister, Rachael, and her husband." He pointed to large framed portrait of a happy-looking couple and three small children.

"Do they live near here?"

A shadow passed over Dex's face. "Rachael passed away almost five years ago. Her husband, too. Car accident."

"Oh. I'm sorry. Those poor kids."

He swallowed. "Yeah. I would love to bring them here to live. They love the ranch and I've always been involved in their lives. But I'm on the road so much right now...they live with my folks, but they're getting older." He looked vaguely ashamed. "My lifestyle isn't the ideal environment for kids."

"I guess not."

I ran my hands over the spines of the books lining his shelves. "This really is amazing."

"Bet you didn't even think I could read."

I shrugged. "It's not that. I just wasn't expecting this when you offered to show me upstairs."

He stepped closer to me and his scent washed over me, the ultimate aphrodisiac. His melancholy was gone. "Did you think I'd take you straight to my bedroom, Miss Stratton?"

He tucked a tendril of hair behind my ear.

I was mesmerized by his dark gaze and sexy half smile and swallowed a lump in my throat before I could answer. "Well, given our last two encounters –"

"Three." Dex traced the line of my jaw. "I know. You're just too damn beautiful. Whenever I'm around you, that's all I can think about." The way he was he was looking at my lips, I was sure he was going to kiss me and since my hormones were already ratcheted up, expecting to go into overdrive at any second, that would have been okay.

But instead, he stepped back. "That's why I'm on my best behavior tonight." He took my hand again. "I want to get to know you better. Outside the bedroom." He grinned. "Or the shower."

Before I could answer the intercom crackled, making me jump a little. "Dinner is ready, Mr. Wilder."

Dex walked over and hit the button on the intercom speaker near the door. "Thanks, Marcy. We'll be right down."

Dex turned to me. "Are you hungry?"

* * * *

Dinner was served on the stone terrace overlooking a small lake. It was fully dark now and moonlight reflected on the tiny waves made by the light breeze. Boats bobbed lightly, moored to docks jutting out into the water. The air had cooled a bit, which was a good thing. Summer here was hot, and even at night, it wasn't uncommon for the temperature to be in the nineties, with enough humidity to choke a Northern girl like me.

Dex had gone all out with the romance. We sat at a small round table covered with a white tablecloth and lit with candles. Expensive wine chilled in a silver ice bucket on a small folding stand next to us. The stereo system had speakers on the terrace, so the music he'd turned on inside filtered softly through night breeze.

He helped me to my chair, then took his own as a slender middle-aged woman brought out our dinner.

"This is Marcy. She cooks for me when I'm home and keeps the place in one piece when I'm not."

"Nice to meet you, Marcy," I said as she set a plate of chicken, corn on the cob and green beans in front of me.

"Nice to meet you, too, Miss. I've heard a few things about you." She glanced at Dex and smiled maternally. "First time Dex has had a date out to the house."

I was a little surprised. "Really? I figured this place was party central when Dex was home."

Dex shook his head. "I like it quiet. I have friends over now and then, but even then, it's not really what you'd call a party."

Marcy set a basket of fresh-baked rolls in front of me. "You two save room for dessert, now. I made Dex's favorite apple pie."

Dex groaned. "You're going to kill me, Marcy."

She patted him on the shoulder with a smile. "Do you want me to close the gate?"

"No, I'll get it when Sydney leaves. Thanks."

Marcy went back into the house and Dex grabbed a glass carafe out of the ice bucket on the stand next to the table. "Sweet tea?"

I nodded and he filled my glass. "What, no champagne?" I teased, remembering the first time we'd met. "Or maybe you're still a beer guy?"

"I don't drink much these days."

"Really? Seems like every picture I see of you, you have a beer in your hand."

"Don't believe everything you see," he said, filling his own glass. "I decided the beer was becoming too big a habit, so I stopped." He put the carafe back into the ice. "But the tour is sponsored by a beer company, so there's always plenty around for photo ops."

"Bet the boys at the brewery didn't like it that their party boy had gone dry."

"They don't know." Dex put his napkin in his lap and smiled across the table at me. "It's our secret."

I smiled back. This Dex was so unlike the one I'd seen in all the tabloids that it was hard to remember they were the same guy.

We ate and talked about everything and nothing at all. We talked about his family a lot and mine a little. We talked about our mutual passion for music, the thing that really tied us together. Of course, he was talking about people he played with regularly on the road and hung out with at various parties and charity events. I was talking about the same people, but I'd only seen them on their album covers and heard them on the radio.

After we finished eating I went to the railing of the terrace. The steps leading down to the lake were lit by little lanterns snaking all the way down.

"Want to take a walk?" Dex asked me, nodding towards the lake.

"Sure."

"Bring your glass." He grabbed his guitar. "And you might want to take those off, unless you want a broken neck," he said, nodding to my four-inch heels.

I happily kicked off my shoes and we made our way down the stone steps to the water's edge. Lights from the neighboring homes reflected in shimmery golden splashes on the water's surface. It was even cooler down here and I shivered a little.

Dex led the way to a swing at the end of his dock.

"This is nice," I said as I sat down on the plush cushions covering the wooden swing's seat.

Dex sat next to me. His thigh was warm against mine and I sipped my tea and looked out over the lake. The sky was black, with only a sliver of moon and a handful of stars to punctuate the darkness. I was incredibly aware of the body next to mine.

"Yeah. Wish I was home more."

"It must be hard to be on the road so much. I've always kind of been a homebody."

He nodded. "Me, too. Well, until this whole music thing sort of exploded."

"Still, it must be fun to go to all those new places. Stay in fancy hotels. See the sights."

Dex smiled. "The only thing I really get to see is the venue we're playing and the inside of the bus. And I can tell you, that gets old fast. Backstage looks the same whether you're in Atlanta or Denver or San Francisco."

"Good thing you have lots of company to liven things up."

I heard the frown in his voice. "Company?"

"Come on. That bus has a revolving door for groupies that flock to your show."

"I told you, you shouldn't believe everything you read."

"Oh, there's no reading involved. Pictures are worth a thousand words."

Dex shook off his frown and brought my hand to his lips. "Jealous?"

I gave him a look but it was hard to concentrate when his warm breath skimmed my knuckles. "No. Why would I be?"

Okay, so maybe I was. A little. But it wasn't as if I had any right to be. I mean, so we'd had sex. Big deal. I wasn't his girlfriend and he definitely was not my boyfriend. He was Dex Wilder, for cryin' out loud.

"Wishful thinking, I guess," he said, and pressed a kiss to the back of my hand.

"You *want* me to be jealous?"

He looked at me with that crooked grin and instantly the chemistry between us that was always at a low boil heated up a notch. Or two.

"Maybe. A little."

"Why?"

He turned my hand over and kissed my palm. A spark ran up my arm.

"Maybe it wouldn't seem so one-sided."

It was hard to follow his line of thinking because he was now kissing my wrist. His tongue darted out to taste the hot pulse points and I wondered if he could tell how fast the blood was rushing just beneath the skin there.

"What's one-sided?"

He stopped kissing my hand and locked gazes with me. The lights lining the walkway and the dock glinted in his dark eyes and he leaned close.

"I like you, Sydney. I think about you. A lot."

I swallowed and shifted on the seat. I decided to play it cool. "I think about you, too." I ran put my hand on the front of his shirt and back down. I gave him a wicked grin so that there was no mistaking exactly what I meant. My hand drifted lower.

He caught my wrist before it reached his waistband. "It's more than that, though, Sydney. At least for me." He dropped my hand and looked out over the lake. "You're a beautiful woman. At first it was just that physical attraction that drew me to you."

He looked over at me. "But there's more. When I'm with you, I feel relaxed. Calm. More like myself than I have in a long time."

"Well, that's good."

He smiled. "Not even going to throw me a bone, here?"

I shook my head. I wasn't exactly sure what he wanted me to say. That I thought about him a lot too? That when it was us, like this, I liked him too? That the whole thing scared the hell out of me? "Not a chance."

"Well, I'll just have to try harder, then, won't I?"

He reached down and grabbed his guitar. "This baby has never failed me."

I laughed lightly. "I'll bet. Girls always go for a guy with a guitar."

Moving to the edge of the swing, he strummed softly at first. Then his deep, smooth voice merged with the tinkling notes and he hummed a melody low and deep. With just his voice and his music and the night, it wasn't long before I stopped laughing and fell completely under his spell.

It wasn't a song I'd heard before. The tune was soft and kind of bittersweet, even without the words. Not his style at all. But it was moving and beautiful and felt like it really came from the heart.

When he finished, he looked up at me and for the first time, I saw something other than utter confidence in the tilt of his mouth and the expression in his eyes.

"What did you think?" He fiddled with the shoulder strap.

CMA's entertainer of the year, double-platinum, new artist award winner and fan favorite was nervous. It blew my mind.

"Did you write it?"

He shrugged. "It's something I've been playing with. I haven't played it for anyone else yet."

"Well," I said, trying to determine the significance of that statement, "it's not your style."

"No."

"I like it."

He set his guitar down against the swing's frame. "You don't have to say –"

"No. I mean, I really like it."

"Really?"

I turned to face him, folding one leg up on the swing. "It's got a great melody. It's not a ballad, exactly, but sweet. Still full of energy, too. Are there words?"

He smiled then. "Not yet. Actually, I had an ulterior motive for asking you here tonight. And not the one your naughty little mind is picturing. Well, not only that one," he said, grinning now. "I listened

to your tape. You have a real talent for lyrics, Syd. I was hoping…
you might help me out on this new piece."

A little thrill shot through me. "I don't know if I can," I said. "I
mean, I'm not a professional or anything. Any songwriter in Nashville would jump at the chance to work with Dex Wilder."

"I don't want a professional. I want you. You're good, Sydney.
And we have a connection. I feel comfortable with you."

He looked out over the lake. "I've never told anyone here about
my sister. But you, you make me feel so at ease, like I've known you
forever. It's…easier to open up to you."

In a flash, I realized why every song Dex Wilder ever sang was
about beer or parties or his favorite pair of boots. As much as a bad
boy and a risk-taker and a successful artist as he was, he was afraid
to show what was on the inside. It all made sense now. And suddenly I did feel close to him.

"Okay."

He turned back to me. "You'll do it?"

"I'll try. Just don't expect too much."

He leaned in then and kissed me. Given what we'd shared in that
public park two years earlier, in his dressing room and even over the
phone, it was a really innocent kiss. Tame and almost chaste. But it
was far more intimate than any of the things we'd shared without
our clothes.

He pulled back and smiled at me. "Thank you." He held my gaze for a minute, then grabbed his guitar again. "I was thinking about something like this for the bridge."

* * * *

Six hours and an apple pie later, we had two verses and a chorus of Dex Wilder's first non-party song. We had moved inside around midnight and were sitting in his library. I had moved to sit on the floor with my back against the couch. He sat on the couch with his guitar next to me, his knee bumping my shoulder every now and then.

It turned out to be a song about a summer love, sweet and bitter-sweet too, but still upbeat and hopeful, just like his music. He came up with some fabulous lines and really, I just added to and expanded the images he'd created, once I saw where he was going with it.

It was easy once I closed my eyes and pictured one particular summer night when the excitement and passion of a summer fling came flooding back. I didn't ask what Dex was thinking of when he wrote the music. I probably didn't want to know. I was sure it wasn't the same image of a cowboy and a girl in a toga that I was thinking of.

Even though I could never be in a room and not be aware of Dex as a man, the creative energy had sapped the desire to jump his bones for once, and the words came more easily than I thought they would. We were a good team. He played, I wrote, and we tried different words, different keys and combinations until everything sort of came together as a whole and I knew we'd nailed it. Dex did, too.

"I think the label is going to love this." Dex said. "I've been wanting to branch out, try something different."

"The regular stuff seems to be paying pretty well," I pointed out. "This is great. But it's a risk."

"It's not about the money. It's about getting back to the reason I fell in love with music in the first place."

I stopped scribbling and looked over at him.

"I didn't grow up easy," he said quietly. "I didn't get along with my folks and got in trouble a lot. Music was always there when I was pissed about something. It was an outlet. An expression. A way to get out what I was feeling."

I nodded. "I know what you mean." The geography was different but he could have described my teen years. The disconnect between me and my parents, the way music was always somewhere I could escape to. The reason I'd moved to a city five hundred miles from home, where I had known nothing and no one.

"I've gotten away from that these last few years," Dex said. "That connection. I still love music, but it's become more of a job than a joy. I feel like I've lost touch with what drew me to it in the first place."

"Well, I think you're off to good start." I smiled up at him.

I could see the first light of dawn peeking through the wooden blinds on the tall window of his library. We'd stayed up all night. And were both still fully clothed. But I hadn't had much sleep the day before and my eyes were starting to burn. I stifled a yawn and rubbed at the tension in my neck.

"Tired?"

"Yeah. Getting there."

Dex set his guitar down and moved behind me so that I was sitting between his knees. He kneaded my shoulders in firm, deep strokes with his big, warm hands.

"God. That feels good."

"I aim to please," he said.

He massaged my shoulders until the tension had disappeared. My eyes drooped and I let my head fall to the side and rested my cheek on his knee. Dex stopped kneading my shoulders and stroked my hair, running his fingers through the long strands. It was relaxing and comfortable, though if I hadn't been completely exhausted, I would have jumped his bones right then.

"Come here, baby."

Dex leaned over and practically lifted me up to the couch beside him. He grabbed the throw from the back of the sofa and setting me against him, covered us with the soft blanket.

He hummed softly under his breath and pressed a kiss to my forehead.

"I should go home," I said, fighting sleep. "I have to work tomorrow. Today. Whatever." I yawned again.

"What time?"

"Um, noon."

"I'll make sure you're up," Dex said, stroking my hair. "Just relax for a couple of hours, okay? I don't want you driving home so tired. What would I do if I lost my co-writer?"

I smiled and snuggled into Dex's warmth. "'kay."

But I didn't get to sleep very long at all.

I woke up when Dex shifted me off his lap and went to answer the intercom.

"Mr. Wilder. There's a situation outside," I heard.

I sat up, rubbing my eyes. "What? What's going on?"

Dex peeked through the window of the library that faced the front of the house. Then he looked back at me. He wasn't smiling.

Holding my gaze, he hit the button on the intercom. "Marcy, please call the police."

Chapter Six

I DRAGGED myself off the couch, wrapping the blanket, still warm from our bodies, around me. I stumbled to the window. Outside was a swarm of reporters, and photographers were crowding around my car and the house.

"Damn it. I left the gate open last night."

"What do they want?"

Dex turned to me ran hand through his hair. "They probably want to know if I'm acknowledging my love child and if I plan to support the baby."

"What?"

Dex walked to the couch and sat down. It was the first time I'd seen him genuinely angry. "Remember that crazy woman in Tulsa?"

"Yeah. The one who thought she was your wife."

Dex nodded. "Turns out she's pregnant and told everybody the baby is mine." He rubbed his eyes. "My publicist told me yesterday she was running her mouth to the press but I told him not to worry about it. That no one would believe her and it would all blow over."

"It didn't." I wrapped the blanket more tightly around me.

"No."

I'd seen the woman on television. She looked like a lot of his other conquests—tall, blond, big boobs. If he'd slept with her... *"Could it be yours?"*

He looked up at me, shocked at first. Then his mouth tightened into a thin line. "No."

I shrugged. "I mean, if it is, it's okay. It's not like you and me... well, it's none of my business."

"The baby is not mine," Dex said through gritted teeth.

"But how can you be sure? I mean –"

"Sydney." Dex stood and stalked over to me, wrapping his hands around my shoulders. "It's not mine. You need to believe me here."

I wanted to believe him. I really did. But I'd seen the tabloids. I'd read about the wild nights spent on the road with anonymous women who looked just like the alleged baby-momma. Dex Wilder had a reputation. And it seemed his partying, free-wheeling lifestyle had just landed him in family court. No wonder the press wanted a piece of him. Nashville's charming, all-American bad boy had just fallen off his throne.

Sirens blared through the early morning quiet as two squad cars pulled up, scattering the throng of reporters and photographers.

"I'm going to have to go talk to them," he said, tucking in his wrinkled blue shirt and smoothing his hair. The trademark scruff was starting to reemerge along his jaw line and apart from the frown marring his full lips and chasing away his ready grin, he looked like the Dex Wilder I'd known before last night. He was back to looking like his poster and living up to his reputation. The guy I'd spent time with, talking and laughing and writing music with, had disappeared.

"Oh, sure. I need to get going anyway." I folded the blanket and put it back on the sofa. "Do you have my tape?"

"Over there, on the table," he said, looking out the window again.

The police were herding the photographers out through the front gate, but that didn't stop them from snapping pictures as they left.

I grabbed the tape and my shoes and headed towards the door. I could only imagine what my hair and clothes looked like, let alone my makeup. It probably looked like I'd had a wild night in Dex Wilder's bed, like countless other women he'd met on the road. It didn't matter. I was just heading home and wouldn't see anyone anyway.

Dex and I went downstairs. "Be careful, Sydney," he said as he walked to the front door with me. "They probably have your license plate number by now. If anyone shows up at your apartment, call the cops." He smiled faintly. "Or just come back here."

I shook my head. "I'll be fine. But thanks anyway."

Dex opened the front door and walked me to my car. The police officers were escorting the last of the camera-wielding maniacs down the driveway towards the front gate.

"This didn't exactly end like I'd planned," he said while I dug my keys out of my purse.

"Yeah." I unlocked my car and Dex opened the door for me. "I had a good time, though." Well, until I'd found out he'd most likely fathered a love child.

"Me, too." He caught my arm before I could duck into the car and pressed me into the side of the car with his big, hot body. Even though I was disturbed by what I'd learned, my libido wasn't. My breath caught at the contact and he gave me one of those irresistible smiles before lowering his mouth to mine and taking my breath away with his kiss.

He loved my mouth slowly, thoroughly, until I could barely breathe. I dropped my shoes and wrapped an arm around his neck. Dex grunted lightly and deepened the kiss, using his tongue to caress all the sensitive places in my mouth until pleasure hummed through my veins and I was seriously considering heading right back inside with him. I could feel how much he was enjoying the kiss, too.

He broke away, smiling. "Now, *that's* a good morning kiss," he said. "Are you sure you can't stay?" He nudged against me, just in case I hadn't felt his arousal the first time. I had. Boy, had I.

"We could cancel what we have going on today and spend the day playing hooky." Dex flicked my hair back from my neck and whispered in my ear. "I haven't even shown you my bedroom." He set his talented mouth to work on the sensitive part of my neck, just below my ear. I tilted my head to the side and let him.

His other hand eased up my thigh and under my skirt. But he stopped with a groan. "The cops. I forgot about the cops."

He pulled away and just as he did, a lone photographer darted from behind the line of hedges by the driveway and sprinted down the gravel drive like the devil was on his heels.

"Shit," Dex said, staring after him. His muscles tensed, and I had the feeling if I wasn't holding on to him, and if he didn't have an erection the size of a fence post, he would be chasing that rascal down.

The police were driving back up from the gate and Dex let me go.

I took the opportunity to slip into the driver's seat before I changed my mind and decided to stay.

"I'll call you," he said, leaning in the window for another quick kiss.

"Okay." The promise gave me a thrill I couldn't quite describe. Did I want him to call me? Was I going to do this thing with him?

Make this more than a one-night stand? I didn't know, but now that I'd seen the other side of Dex, the part he'd kept hidden from the world, I was leaning at least a little towards the yes column.

He stroked my cheek and I leaned my face against his warm palm. "Be careful, Sydney. Promise me you'll call if you have any problems."

* * * *

A few days after my night at Dex's, I discovered I had problems. Big problems.

Pictures started to surface in all the trashiest tabloids first. They were blurry and if I hadn't known, I wouldn't have been able to tell it was me in the photos of us outside by my car. But eventually, as Dex predicted, someone traced my license plates and my name began showing up in the captions. Then names not as nice showed up with it. Names like "Wilder's New Plaything" and "Bimbo *du jour.*"

It was mortifying, seeing myself all rumpled with Dex's hands up my skirt, looking like we'd just spent a night rolling around in his sheets, or were about to do it right there against my car. Of course, the worst part was that we hadn't done anything but have a beautiful dinner, write a kick-ass love song and fall asleep on the couch together like an old married couple. But that didn't sell papers, so I was the new Wilder Woman, and wasn't it just like a man to knock one woman up and be ho-ing around with another one back in Nashville? That's what all the magazines said, anyway.

"Here's a new one," Becca said, as I was pouring coffee into a gigantic "I Hate Monday" mug. It wasn't Monday.

I turned and glared at the newest magazine cover Becca was holding. I had always wanted to be on the cover of a magazine, but for my music, not looking like the slut of the week. I peeked out the tiny kitchen window over the sink. There were already two or three guys with cameras milling about on the sidewalk. It had been a week since the fateful dinner. They just didn't give up.

"Man, is he hot."

Becca was drooling over the pictures of Dex in the inside spread detailing the whole nasty scandal of his love child and his new girl-toy.

"Yeah." I sipped my coffee. That's what had gotten me into this in the first place.

She looked up at me. "I don't see why you're so bent out of shape. This is great publicity. You look hot."

"I look like a slut."

She shrugged. "So what? It's Dex Wilder, Sydney. Dex. Wilder."

"I know his name."

Becca put down the paper. "He called again last night."

"So what?" I echoed back at her. Dex was the last person I wanted to talk to.

"It's not his fault, you know."

My anger had cooled considerably since I'd seen the first tabloid picture of myself getting it on with Dex. But I'd decided it was better if we just didn't see each other anymore. In any capacity. With the photographers hanging around my house just waiting for some other juicy photo op, the last thing I needed was to give them a chance for one.

And who knew how many other women were pregnant with his babies? I couldn't live like that, wondering who was going to show up next, baby in tow. No, it was better to nip this, whatever it was, in the bud. If I could just find the strength to ignore his calls, the sad tone in his voice when he left a message asking me to call him, asking if I was okay, surely all these softer feelings just beginning to blossom for him would disappear. It hurt, yes, but not as much as it would a month or two months or a year down the line if I continued to get closer to Dex. But I didn't feel like explaining all that to Becca.

"I know," I said. "I just think it's better this way."

She shook her head. "You're nuts. He's hot. Think what he could do for your career. No more Willie's Wagon Wheel."

"I'm not *sleeping* my way to a record deal," I said, truly angry now. That's what some of the tabloids had suggested once someone found out about me and Road Kill.

"Yeah, but it's helping. How packed was the Chug last night?"

It was full. Standing room only. But a lot of those present had cameras and were not there for the music. The guys in the band loved it. They had no problem whoring me out for a few more fans and another couple of bookings.

"Oh, this came for you in the mail." Becca handed me a plain white envelope with a record company's logo as the return address. Great, another rejection. Just what I needed to really make this day perfect. I should just save myself the trouble and toss it in the garbage unopened.

I ripped the envelope open anyway and read the letter.

My hands started to shake. "Oh. My. God."

"What?" Becca circled behind me to read over my shoulder. "Sydney! You did it! You made the cut!"

She hugged me and I read the letter again just to be sure it wasn't some kind of joke.

I'd sent in my demo tape the previous week and then I hadn't thought about it much. I'd been a little preoccupied dodging photographers and phone calls from a multi-platinum-selling suitor.

"This says I have to perform live on Saturday morning for the panel of judges."

"Oh my God! This is great!" Becca hugged me. "See? Knowing Dex is helping."

I frowned. My blood ran cold. "I hope it's because they liked my demo, not because of the tabloid photos."

"What does it matter? I mean, I'm sure they liked the demo, but think about it. If Dex Wilder's girlfriend wins, they've got built-in publicity for the contest and for your first album."

I frowned. Becca had a point. And I'd had enough dealing with these record guys to know they were totally mercenary. They weren't above using a gimmick or a tabloid photo or a celebrity connection to sell records.

"What are you going to wear?" Becca asked, returning to her cornflakes and the tabloid on the table. "I think you need to go out and buy something really killer. Show some cleavage."

"Oh, I think there's plenty of my cleavage floating around already," I said, refolding the letter and putting it back in the envelope.

Becca turned the page of the magazine. "Oh, a new one! Wait. That's not you." She squinted at the small inset photo in the layout of the article.

I looked over her shoulder. "No. It's not." The woman was blond and was kissing Dex, but she wasn't me. There were several photos in the layout of Dex kissing tall blond girls, none of whom was me. Clearly, I was just one in a long line of tabloid honeys, as the magazine pointed out. I wondered if one of those women was the one having Dex's love child.

I shrugged and tightened the belt on my ratty old robe. "Dex can make out with whomever he wants. It's none of my business."

Becca looked over her shoulder at me. "And you're not jealous. Not even a tiny bit."

"No," I lied. "Not a bit."

The phone rang and I had a sinking feeling I knew who it was. I checked the caller ID anyway. Yep. Dex.

"You aren't even going to throw the poor guy a bone?"

"I think he's got plenty of other bones," I said, nodding towards the tabloid. "He doesn't need mine."

"But how much do you need his?" Becca grinned.

I rolled my eyes. "I have to go. I've got to find a new outfit. Sans cleavage."

Dex didn't leave a message and I was almost disappointed. I wanted to hear his voice again, even though I knew what I was doing was for the best. It had to be this way. It was the only way I could accomplish what I'd come to Nashville to do. I didn't want the distraction. I needed to refocus my energies on something besides Dex Wilder. The tabloid photos would go away as soon as Dex found another blonde to snuggle up to.

I had a contest to win.

Chapter Seven

NASHVILLE LIES smack in the middle of the Bible Belt, and the Ryman Auditorium is the most conspicuous monument to the city's religious past. Built in 1892 to host revivals, the place has church pews for seats and gorgeous stained glass windows, all original to the building. The Grand Ole Opry started there in the '40s and moved to a more commercially viable location in the '70s.

But the Ryman is famous for more than country music. Everybody from Marian Anderson to Will Rogers, Elvis to Larry the Cable Guy have trod the boards at the old theater, and there's a sense of reverence that overtakes you as soon as you enter and see all the pictures of past performers gracing the walls. It was built as a monument to God, but today it's a monument to music, and it's every singer's dream to stand there, on the old scarred, wooden boards, and play to a packed house.

That's where the contest semi-finals took place. As if there wasn't enough pressure to perform without thinking about freakin' Elvis having played the same stage.

The Ryman is on 5th Avenue, only a few blocks from my ratty apartment, and even though there was a light drizzle, I decided to walk to the auditorium and try to get some of the nervous, fluttery feeling out of my belly before I had to perform. There were a couple of photographers snapping pictures, but I was getting adept at ignoring them, and I concentrated instead on my song on the walk over.

I went in through the front doors, and after the greeter made sure my name was on the list, I was directed to the green room. He kicked the photographers out, telling them it was a closed audition. My new hero.

The green room was a zoo. Twenty-five singer-songwriters milled about, most looking like they were going to toss their cookies at any moment.

I took my wet jacket off and looked around the room. Some of the faces were ones I recognized from the bar circuit. I smiled at one redheaded girl I'd hung out with on occasion, but she looked away quickly without returning my greeting and I became aware of the whispers and stares of several people there.

I could only assume they had seen the tabloids. Great.

Now I was the slut sleeping her way to the top: no judge, no jury, just execution. It hurt, but facing constant criticism and rejection for more than two years had made my skin tough. So what if a bunch of people I really didn't know thought something about me that totally wasn't true? It shouldn't bother me, but it did, and I could feel my face burning under their stares.

With no one to talk to, I pulled out a notebook and jotted down a line or two that had been running through my head on the way over. It had promise. Not surprisingly, it was about truth and lies and about how easy it is to mix up the two. Imagine that. I ignored the eyes burning into the back of my head and lost myself in the music as I always did when things got rough.

Eventually a harried-looking assistant with a clipboard rushed into the room.

"Good, you're all here now. Here's how this thing is going to work. We'll call you in one at a time, and you'll do your song for the judges. Each judge will give his or her critique and score. The top ten scorers move on to the finals and the TV special. We'll film that next Saturday. Anybody have questions?"

The assistant answered a few questions, then left the room that was now buzzing with tension and electricity. The first few contestants paced and warmed up their voices. I fidgeted in my chair and tried to concentrate on what I was writing to keep my mind calm.

One by one, people were led from the room by the assistant until just a few of us were left. They were taking us by alphabetical order and as an "S," I was toward the end.

I put away my notebook and checked the clock. It had been over two hours. I stood up and stretched my back. There were only three of us remaining now, including the redhead who had given me the cold shoulder when I'd walked in. That's when she decided to speak to me.

"So did Dex Wilder pull strings to get you here?"

I stared at her, not even knowing how to respond. "No," I said. "I sent in my tape just like you."

"Well, not just like me," she smirked. "I gave my tape to Ron and he turned it in for me."

Ron Lennart. The record producer who'd propositioned me in the bar. Clearly he'd found someone willing to screw him for a chance at stardom.

"Well, congratulations, I guess," I said.

She smiled. "Ron thinks I have talent."

"I'm sure he does," I said under my breath. And the sad thing was, I'd heard the girl sing and she *did* have talent. I couldn't help but feel a little sorry for her for not having the self esteem to see that for herself, to ditch the creep and do it on her own.

I could tell she was peeved that I wasn't more impressed about her sharing the toad's bed. but I didn't have to think up anything else, because it was my turn to perform for the judges.

I'd toured the Ryman before, and been on stage as a tourist. It was one of the first places I'd visited after moving to Nashville and I remembered the feeling now, standing in the same spot. I'd been so full of optimism and hope and pure joy at just being in the Music City that I could hardly stand it.

I still felt like that a lot. But reality had taken hold, too. I was a little disillusioned, but at the end of the day, I had to believe that all I'd gone through and worked so hard for would eventually pay off.

Starting now.

I walked onto the stage and faced the panel of judges, who were sitting in the first row of pews, looking up at me expectantly.

There was a mic and a stool and not much else on the empty stage. The red, blue, and yellow stained glass windows at the rear of the auditorium cast light on the church pews, and suddenly I felt very small up there with nothing but my guitar and my voice.

Each of the judges had a clipboard and a pencil and a look that said they were here for business rather than pleasure. As I looked down the row of faces, I recognized a few of the faces. Some, I didn't. But the last one, I most definitely did.

Ron Lennart was staring at me from the far left, a leering grin on his face. Shit. The redhead's boyfriend recognized me. Remembered me. Still hated me for turning down his sex-for-studio-time swap.

Ignoring the toad, I smiled at the panel and settled on the stool, my guitar cradled in my lap. I adjusted the mic and cleared my throat.

"Whenever you're ready, Miss Stratton. Just do the song you sent in on the tape."

"Okay," I said into the microphone and the sound of my voice echoed throughout the auditorium.

My hands were shaking and sweaty, and it was a good thing I was sitting down. I took a deep breath, smiled at the panel and started my song.

I had played the song so often that the chords came naturally to my fingers. The music was no issue, so I concentrated on the singing, on putting every ounce of emotion I possessed into my voice and hitting the right note and regulating my breathing.

It seemed like forever, but before I knew it, the last notes hung in the air. I'd made it through. I wanted to laugh with relief. Or maybe vomit.

It wasn't a perfect performance, I knew that. But hopefully it was enough. By the time the last chords echoed off the church pews in the top row, a couple of the judges were smiling and nodding as they scribbled notes on their clipboards. A few had no expression at all, and Lennart was grinning evilly and scribbling as if his life depended on it.

I waited.

Finally the head judge smiled. "We'll each give you a little critique now, and then you can go to the lounge with the other contestants, have a bite to eat if you want, and wait for the scores."

I nodded, my throat too dry to form words.

"I thought it was great. I loved the emotion behind the song and the lyrics were really evocative of what it feels like to fall in love. Good job."

My heart lightened at the head judge's praise.

"I thought the voice was a little weak, but the lyrics, as Geoff said, were superb," judge number two said. "Really vivid. They really complemented the relatively simple melody."

One by one, the judges critiqued my song. Some of the comments were hard to hear. Like "overly sentimental" and "simplistic." But more judges than not gave me a lot of positive feedback. And then it was the toad's turn.

"Once again we prove that talent and fame, or should I say infamy, are two different things entirely," he started, speaking loud and clear, as if he was performing a soliloquy. "I hated the lyrics. Your playing was passable, but the overall performance made me want to run screaming from the room. Get some voice lessons if you plan to make it in this town." He paused and narrowed his eyes on me. "Or maybe get yourself in more compromising photos with big country stars. Half the battle in this town is who you're friendly with and what enemies you make."

My face turned red. I know it did. But I wasn't sure if it was shock at Lennart's caustic words, his criticism, the embarrassment at having those photos brought to all the other judges' attention, or whether it was rage, pure and simple, at the outright unfairness of his accusation that I was a slut.

The head judge looked clearly uncomfortable at Lennart's tirade and the other judges were whispering amongst themselves. I knew they all recognized me, now that Mr. Wonderful had pointed out I was the girl in the seedy photos. I wondered how much it would affect the judge's final scores.

"Thank you, Miss Stratton. You can take a break. We'll have the scores and the finalists' names in about half an hour."

"Thank you," I said into the mic and exited the stage, fighting the stinging tears at the back of my eyes.

But besides putting a hit out on Toad Boy, there was nothing I could do now. I'd performed to the best of my ability and would just have to wait to hear the final verdict. Even if I didn't win the thing, just making it to the top ten and being on the CMT special would give my career a serious boost. I took a deep breath and pasted a smile on my face as I headed down the hallowed halls lined with pictures and busts and framed programs from performers past.

Back in the lounge, the tension was crazy. Someone had brought in some coffee and refreshments and some of the contestants were nibbling on cheese and crackers or tiny sandwiches. Some were drinking the coffee like there was no tomorrow and some were pacing in circles, clearly too nervous to eat. I, for one, never passed up a free meal, so I wandered over to the refreshments to have a snack.

It was close to an hour before the results came back. We were each given an envelope and asked not to open it, then we were ushered back on stage to face the judges as a group.

The head judge stood. "I want to thank you all for entering our singer-songwriter contest and let you know the judges had a very difficult time narrowing the field to our top ten finalists."

I shifted my weight. My hands were sweating and the heavy sense of anticipation was almost unbearable.

"That said, we did choose our top ten, based on scores from the panel. Judges gave each performer a score from one to ten and we added up the scores to determine the top ten finalists."

I glanced at Lennart. He was sitting back in his chair, legs crossed, arms folded, looking back at me with a shit-eating grin on his face.

"But you're all really winners," the head judge continued. "You twenty-five semi-finalists were chosen from a field of nearly one thousand entrants from all over the country." He smiled at each of us and I got a good vibe from the guy. He, at least, seemed genuine.

"Categories we looked at were lyrics, musicality, showmanship, voice, and overall impression," he continued.

I shifted my weight, wishing he would just get on with it. Waiting was the hardest part.

"We'll start at the top."

"Amber Green. Please step forward."

The girl squealed and stepped out, positively beaming. I'd heard her perform. She was good.

"Neil Booker." A tall man in cowboy boots stepped out and doffed his hat to the judges.

"Campbell Yardly."

One by one, finalists were called to step forward until nine of the ten had been called. I and the other fifteen contestants chewed lips, shifted from foot to foot and tried to calm racing pulses as we waited for the tenth and final name.

"Ginger Bell."

Another squeal rang out as the redhead stepped forward and hugged one of the other girls. Her roommate. How convenient.

Disappointment washed over me as I realized my dream of making it to the finals, winning the whole thing, and being signed by a record label had just crashed and burned. And I had a sneaking suspicion why.

"Thanks again to everyone who participated. Your individual scores are in the envelopes you've been given. We'll need the finalists to stick around so we can tell you about the rehearsal schedule and the television special."

All of us losers exited the stage. Some of the rejected cursed. Some claimed foul play. All shuffled dejectedly back to the green room to collect jackets and instruments and head home. Or to a bar.

I went home and cut through the photographers lingering on my doorstep without a word. I went straight upstairs, poured myself a tall glass of white zin and deleted the two new messages Dex had left on my machine without listening to them.

* * * *

I'm really sorry, Sydney," Dillon said, after he'd moved his amp into place on the small stage at The Tap later that night. "That sucks."

I smiled at him. He really was a nice guy. And I'd bet he didn't have a pregnant blonde in some faraway city. But I wasn't thinking about you-know-who anymore.

"Thanks, Dillon."

"It sounds like some of the judges really liked your stuff. Maybe you should send something out to some of them."

I shrugged. For two years I'd picked myself up off the ground. With each rejection, each setback, I'd given myself the never-quit pep talk. I'd reminded myself that all the big stars went though tough times but kept with it to get where they were. Where I wanted to be.

That night, it wasn't working. I was over it. I was tired. And pissed. I kept wondering if those pictures had never surfaced, if I had never gone to Dex's house that night, never hooked up with him to begin with, whether things would have turned out differently with the contest. I'd what-iffed myself into a monster headache and the last thing I felt like doing was performing. But I was a professional and professionals didn't ditch gigs because they'd had their feelings hurt.

"You should try some music publishers. You're a great writer."

I smiled at Dillon, who was trying so hard to be helpful. "Maybe I will."

"Want us to kick the shit out of that record guy, Syd?" Ted asked. He wasn't the sharpest tool in the shed, but he was earnest. And I knew he enjoyed a good bar fight.

"No. But thanks, Ted. That's really sweet."

He winked at me. "You know we got your back, babe."

We finished setting up and went to the bar for a quick refreshment. Our set didn't start for another fifteen minutes. I looked around. It was a Tuesday night and the place was dead, as usual. This was going to be another stellar show, I could tell.

I sipped my Corona and looked around the dingy, smoky room and wondered how my dream had gotten so off track. I mean, I didn't spend all those years fantasizing about playing shit holes like this for a dozen drunk rednecks and only slightly more pay than free drinks. Maybe it was time to give it up and find a real job. Just the thought of crawling back home to Indiana as a complete failure made me shudder. Though one was usually my limit, I asked for a second Corona and drank that one, too.

The guys talked and joked with the cute bartender in cut off jeans and skimpy T-shirt rolled up and tucked under her prominent and braless breasts. Sheesh. Bet *she* went home with a lot of tips. Maybe I should see if they were hiring.

Road Kill went on stage at ten on the dot, not that anyone really noticed anything but the drink specials and the bartender's breasts.

I had to dig deep to find the passion, the exhilaration performing usually gave me. Some of our gigs had been much different than this, especially early on. Then, being up on stage, under the lights, singing, playing music I loved, the energy of the crowd, the noise, looking out over the people to see them mouthing my words back at me. It was the adrenaline rush, the fear, the expectation of the whole thing that had made me do this night after night, even when the reaction wasn't as good.

Tonight, I had to fake it. I pasted a smile on my face and in my signature opening, asked the crowd if they were ready to rock. There was no answer, just a couple of semi-glazed looks towards the stage from the half-buzzed clientele.

I sang our opening number. The band sounded good tonight. Maybe it was the beer beginning to relax me and force a feeling of warmth and well being through my veins, but by the end of the second song, one I'd written about a cheating boyfriend, I had perked up a little. By the fourth, I was having a good time and feeling the buzz from the music as much as the beer and the adrenaline.

The crowd had grown, too, and the place was filling up. I wondered if people were there to see us. Maybe our music was finally attracting a few followers. Then I looked out over the growing crowd and saw the one face I had been avoiding.

Dex was sitting in the back with his black cowboy hat pulled low over his face. His hands were wrapped around a longneck and he was sitting back in his chair, just staring at me with a small smile on his face.

I skipped a verse of the cover we were doing of a Garth Brooks tune. The band stumbled a little, but thanks to Dillon's quick reaction on guitar, no one noticed and the other two guys followed his lead.

A rush of nerves and awareness washed over me and I forced myself to look somewhere else. I could feel his eyes on me, though, and wondered what the hell he was doing in this dive. He hated going out in public and surely he had better places to be. Other blondes to screw.

I managed to get through two more songs and the guitar solo without looking at Dex. By then, the bar was standing room only. Dex was a magnet and when I did glance to his side of the bar, I noticed a bunch of people crowding around him, clamoring for autographs. More than a few were hot girls thrusting their chests out, trying to get his attention.

We finished the set with a good bit of applause and came down off the stage. I meant to head straight for the bar for my unheard-of third Corona, but when I saw Dex get up and head my way, I totally chickened out. I made a U-turn and went straight to the ladies' room.

I splashed some cool water on my burning face and tried to catch my breath. My reaction to him was as strong as ever. His showing up here wasn't helping my Forget Dex Wilder campaign. Not at all. And how the hell was I going to get through the second set with him sitting there, staring at me and looking totally hot?

A toilet flushed and the hot bartender came out and washed her hands at the sink next to me.

"Great set tonight, Sydney. You guys are rocking the place!"

I smiled weakly. "Thanks." I dried my face and pulled out the eyeliner and powder I kept stashed in my back pocket to touch up my makeup.

"Did you see who was out there?" she asked, drying her hands.

"Yeah. I saw."

"I read that the two of you –"

"Don't believe everything you read," I snapped. I immediately felt bad and turned to smile at her sheepishly. "Sorry. Bad subject."

She grinned back. "No worries. Men are a pain in the butt no matter how famous they are, aren't they?"

A look into her blue eyes told me she was speaking from experience. "Yeah. They're all jerks."

"Amen to that," she grinned and tucked her shirt a little tighter under her boobs. "See you out there."

The door closed behind her. The jukebox blared a Big and Rich song, the bathroom door only slightly muffling the music and excited murmur of the crowd.

I closed my eyes and leaned on the counter, trying to regain my composure. I had to go back on stage in fifteen minutes and freaking out over some guy in the audience wasn't helping.

The door opened and closed and I packed up my makeup without looking at the woman who entered.

Until I discovered it wasn't a woman.

"Sydney," Dex said from behind me.

I spun around. "What are you doing in here? You can't come in –"

But he'd crossed the distance between us and was kissing my lips with as much passion and need and pent-up desire as was coursing through my own veins. I had a lot of will power but not where Dex was concerned. It had been hard to resist him on the phone. It was impossible to resist him in person.

I gave in and wrapped my arms around his neck.

He tasted like beer and desire and he was wearing a hint of the earthy, musky cologne that mixed with his own scent and drove me out of my mind.

I heard the door open and a small squeak of surprise before it slammed shut again.

Dex raised his head. He reached behind him to flip the lock on the door and set his hat on the counter before taking up where he'd left off.

Dex wrapped me tightly in his arms and I made no complaint when he slid his tongue into my mouth and brought me hard up against his body, his hands on my backside.

Desire surged through me, stronger than it had ever been. I clutched at him, too, moaning into his mouth. My hands roamed over his shoulders, across his flexed biceps, down to his hips. To the fly straining with the effort to contain his hard-on.

This time it was him who groaned. He pulled away and stared into my eyes. I stared back and no words were necessary. In a flash, his pants were around his knees, my panties were a memory and I was sitting on the countertop. Dex sheathed himself and was buried deep inside me before I could even think better of making out in a bar bathroom or think about all the people who were no doubt gathered outside, listening. I just didn't care.

The only thing that mattered was Dex kissing my throat, touching me, making me crazy.

It was hot and hard and rough with no words, no lingering caresses, just an expression of the need that had built up over the last few weeks. I wrapped my legs around his waist and went with it.

We were breathing too hard to even attempt kissing, so I buried my face in his neck and clutched at his damp hair as tension coiled tighter and tighter inside me. Blood surged though my veins until I felt lightheaded and I bit at his neck in a show of purely primal need.

He groaned my name and that was the last push I needed to send me soaring over the edge. My body clenched and released, waves of pleasure overtaking me. I cried out, the sound echoing off the tiled walls.

His answering release was just as loud and he shuddered, pulsing deep inside me.

We stayed there for a moment, just breathing and clinging to each other. The sound of the packed bar drifted back to me and the horror of what just happened sunk in. Great. This would give the tabloids a new bit of gossip. I just hoped there weren't any security cameras in the john. I really didn't care to star in my own porno.

Dex must have felt my withdrawal and pulled back a little to look at me.

"Why didn't you call me?" He looked genuinely upset.

I swallowed. "Dex, I don't think –"

He swooped in for another mind-numbing kiss, then pulled back. "Why didn't you call me?" he asked again, softer this time.

I tried to pull back. I needed space. But his arms were clamped around me like a vise. "I don't think –"

Another kiss cut off the words he didn't want to hear.

He pulled back and arched a brow, waiting.

"Fine. I was scared. And angry."

He kissed me lightly and stepped back.

He cleaned up and by the time he was re-buttoned, I was too.

"I'm sorry," he said simply. "I'm sorry you got pulled into all this." He ran a hand through his damp hair. "I know how it is at first, dealing with the constant attention. Especially when not all of it is good."

I rolled my eyes and washed my hands. "Oh, right. You show up in a photo with a bevy of blondes and you're the stud-muffin hero of guys everywhere. I'm in *one* photo and suddenly I'm a whore. The new Wilder Girl."

I shut off the water and dried my hands.

Dex touched my arm. "I know, Sydney. I'm sorry."

"That doesn't help anything, though, does it? It doesn't take all those rags off the stand. It doesn't keep my mother from calling, wanting to know what the hell I'm doing. It doesn't keep the leers, the side looks, the snide comments away."

I glared at him, narrowing my eyes with all the humiliation and anger and hurt I'd felt the past week over the pictures, over the contest, over the frustration of not making it in Nashville. "Does it make me anything than just another groupie you screw in the back of your party bus?" I turned away. "I guess I can at least be glad *I'm* not having your bastard. We can just walk away now and forget it ever happened."

I turned towards the door, but Dex was standing there. He was angry now. Well and truly angry.

"No. You're not going to end it. Not like this." He ran his hands through his hair again and it made me feel marginally better seeing his usual composure so rattled.

"I know this isn't easy. Being with me and all the crap I put up with on a daily basis won't be any easier. But we have something here, Sydney. You are so much more than some woman in a tabloid photo." He looked away, still frowning, then leveled his gaze on me again. "I care about you. Sydney. The other night at the house was great. I just feel like I know you. That you know me in a way I haven't ever connected with another person, and that I get you in the same way."

Some of the anger had faded from his face. "I think you feel the same."

I shook my head. "It's too much, Dex. I don't want to be just another girl in a photo. I have aspirations of my own, you know, and it's not to be your good-time girl. There are plenty of women out there who would be more than happy to fulfill that role."

He stepped closer to me and held my upper arms loosely, forcing me to look up into his familiar features. "Damn it, Syd. Listen to me. I don't want a good-time girl. I want you." He leaned in to kiss me, but I turned my head at the last minute and his lips brushed my cheek.

It was too much. Too tempting. Too much potential for heartbreak. Too much possibility for complete and total destruction. "Right. Until you go back out on the road and I see new photos of you and some woman you knocked up."

He let me go and stepped back.

Someone pounded on the bathroom door. "Hey! You can't lock the door," a slurred voice shouted through the beat-up door with generations of "Bobby + Sue" type messages carved into the wood.

"I have to go," I said, my gaze never leaving his.

"At least talk to me. After the show. We can go back to your place."

I chewed my lip. "I don't think that's a good idea." I'd be naked within a millisecond of hitting the door.

The pounding at the door grew more insistent.

"Please, Sydney, just to talk. If you still decide you don't want me in your life, I'm gone. I won't bother you again."

My heart fell just thinking about it. But it was for the best. I needed to close the door on this and try to figure out what the hell I was doing with my life. The only thing I knew for sure was that playing tabloid queen wasn't it.

"Okay," I said, eyeing the door. "Okay. After the show."

He smiled at me and flipped the lock. "See you then."

He shouldered out of the restroom, past several shocked-looking women. I ran out before anyone could ask me any embarrassing questions and headed back to the stage. I was late for the set and the rest of the band was already waiting for me, warming up.

"You okay, Sydney?" Dillon asked frowning. His eyes followed Dex as he made his way through the horde that now packed the bar and headed out the door into the night.

"I'm fine." I forced a smile. "Now let's get this thing going."

Chapter Eight

I REALLY don't remember the second set. I could have been singing Christmas carols for all I knew. All I could think about was Dex and the fact that he was going to be waiting for me at my apartment when I got home.

I was equal parts terrified, excited, and dreading it all at once. I had to put an end to things once and for all. I knew it and he knew it, too, even if he didn't want to admit it. I wasn't the kind of woman he was used to and I wasn't going to drop everything to chase him around like a fool. I also couldn't see him as a one-woman kind of guy. Not with his busy lifestyle, constant travel and the temptation of women throwing themselves at him wherever he went. Like bar bathrooms.

There were still quite a few people in the club by the time we finished. I had a beer with the band and let the place clear out a little before I headed home as if nothing was going on. If I'd hurried up and gotten out of there, someone would have teased me about having a hot date. All I needed was some photographer to suspect I was meeting Dex and following me home to take more pictures that would be difficult to explain to my mother.

I'd delayed as long as I could, though, and I grabbed my gear and headed towards the door.

"Miss Stratton."

I turned at the sound of my voice. I thought it was probably another reporter, but when I turned, I found it was the head judge from the competition. My heart beat a little faster.

"Yes?"

He walked over to me with a smile on his face. Not a leering, have-sex-with-me-and-I'll-give-you-a-contract smile. Just a smile.

He held out his hand and I shook it. "Geoff Nolan. From the contest."

I nodded. "Nice to see you again."

"You, too. Great set, by the way."

"Thanks. We had a nice crowd tonight." I set my guitar case down.

"I just wanted to let you know that the judges really loved your song at the competition. If there had been eleven spots, you would have been in the finals." He looked away, frowning slightly. "There was one judge who gave you low scores across the board. That's what kept you out."

I knew, of course, who he was talking about. "Yeah."

"I don't know what's between you two and I know it doesn't seem fair. But we had to go by the rules."

I nodded. "I understand." I gave him a small smile. Poor guy. Had he come all the way down here to tell me that? "No hard feelings."

"I really was impressed by your work. I think you've got a real songwriting talent and I'd like to hear more."

"You would?" My breath caught in the back of my throat.

He nodded. "You've got a sort of honesty and plain-spoken style that's appealing. I'm producing a project for a new artist and we need a couple of more songs to complete the album. I'm thinking you might have just what we've been looking for."

I was floored. The type of guy I'd been chasing for two years was now chasing me. I felt lightheaded and grasped the back of a nearby chair for a little extra support.

"Do you have anything else ready?"

I swallowed. "Yeah. I have a couple of things you might like."

"Great. Maybe you could send the lead sheets and lyrics tomorrow?" He pulled out his wallet and handed me his business card.

"Uh, sure." I looked at the card, half expecting to wake up any minute from what was surely a dream.

"Great. I can't wait to see what you've got for me." Mr. Nolan put his wallet back in his back pocket. "And I'm sorry again about what happened this morning."

I shrugged. "No big deal." I put the card in my back pocket. "Thanks again, Mr. Nolan."

"No. Thank you. I'll be in touch. I'm sure of it." He smiled, then left the bar.

"What was that?" Dillon asked, coming up behind me.

I turned and hugged him. He was surprised but wrapped his arms around my waist anyway. "Karma."

* * * *

I was on cloud nine when I left The Tap a few minutes later. I nearly skipped home and even the lone photographer who had waited around for me outside couldn't faze me tonight. The rest of the band had already left and I couldn't wait to tell somebody my big news. I couldn't stop smiling as my mind raced ahead to projects I might want to send Mr. Nolan.

I completely forgot about Dex until I unlocked the door and found him sitting on my raggedy secondhand couch, a glass of sweet tea in his hands.

"Oh. Hi." I said, taking off my coat and locking the door behind me.

"Your roommate let me in," he said, standing up. "She had to go, but said I could wait here for you. I hope that's okay."

"Sure," I said and went to the kitchenette to pour myself a glass of tea.

"You must have had a good set," Dex said, bringing his empty cup to the sink.

"Yeah, it was." I smiled but was unwilling to share my news with him for some reason. It wasn't that I didn't want him to know. It was just that it seemed like such a small thing to a guy who had platinum records, a big-time recording deal, and a house that made my apartment look like some flop house on the wrong side of the tracks. My news was almost embarrassing compared to the level of success he lived with on a daily basis.

I held up the pitcher of tea. "Refill?"

"Sure."

We drank our tea in silence for a few minutes before he spoke.

"Thanks for letting me come up."

I really didn't want to have this conversation, but with renewed confidence still buzzing through my veins, I hoped it would be a little easier.

"Do you want to sit down?" I asked.

We headed back to my ratty sofa and I hoped he hadn't noticed the stains or the odd smell wafting from it. He didn't seem to notice anything but me.

"I'm sorry about what happened at the club," he said, not quite meeting my eyes. "I...when I'm around you, I sort of lose my mind, I guess." He turned to me. "I was so worried when you didn't return my calls. I was afraid something had happened to you."

I knew what he was really getting at. He wanted to know why I hadn't called him back. I didn't answer, just waited as patiently as possible for him to finish what he'd come here to say.

"I meant what I said, Syd. You've come to mean a lot to me."

"I know." I didn't doubt his sincerity. "I just don't see how this can be anything more than what it is."

"And what do you think this is?" he asked, looking at me though narrowed eyes.

I shrugged. "A fling. A good time. A one-night stand...times three."

He looked me for a moment and I could feel myself blush under his assessing gaze. "That's really what you think?"

I didn't feel that way, but I sure wasn't going to offer up my heart in return for his thinking of me as the girl of the week. I had no doubt that he meant what he said about caring about me. I just thought he'd been playing a part for so long, he didn't know what was true in his own heart.

"Yeah. That's what I think."

Dex looked disappointed. "You're wrong."

"Look, Dex. I can tell you're sincere. I believe that you do think you have feelings for me that go beyond crazy bathroom sex. But what happens next week when some other blonde catches your eye? The week after that?"

He shook his head. "No, this is different, Syd. I know it." He looked at his hands. "I've never been able to open up to someone the way I can to you. I can be myself."

He ran a hand through his hair. "There's a reason I've never written my own stuff before. Why I sing songs about beer and women and partying. It's easy. It doesn't take much of yourself to sing that stuff, you know?"

I nodded.

"But the other night, when we were working on that song, something clicked. A door opened and for the first time in a long time, I wasn't afraid to put it all out there."

"It's a good song," I agreed. "I think you need to trust yourself more."

He frowned. "My label doesn't want to hear it."

"What? What do you mean?"

"I played the demo for my producer. He said it was a great song. For somebody else."

"But it's your song."

"Doesn't matter. I have a certain audience that expects certain things. And love songs ain't it."

"That's not fair." It made me mad. We'd worked hard on that song. It was Dex's baby and now he wasn't even going to get to record it.

He shrugged. "That's business."

"What are you going to do?"

"I don't know yet. The label is bound and determined that the song won't be on the album. That people won't accept me as a serious artist. That it would totally flop."

"I don't believe that."

He squeezed my hand and gave me a small smile. "See. You're good for me." He moved in closer and I knew he was about to kiss me. The bathroom scene would look like a church social if that happened. "And I wish you'd let me be good for you."

I leaned away. "I just can't, Dex."

I stood up and paced behind the couch, not trusting myself to be so close to him. "I can't be that girl. No matter how I might feel about you."

"That girl?"

"The girl in the tabloid photo. The girl with you on the red carpet. The eye candy. The trophy wife. The girl who, even if I do make it someday, people will say it's because I'm nailing Dex Wilder."

I stopped and looked at him. "Geoff Nolan came up to me after the show tonight. He heard my song at the contest and wants to see more. He gave me his card."

"Sydney! That's great!" He stood, too.

"But don't you get it? It wasn't because of my looks. Or because I was in a tabloid with a country music star. Or because he thought I was the girlfriend of a rich and powerful force in the industry. It was because of me and what I can do." I shook my head. "It's what I've always wanted. To be seen for who I am and what I can do. Not what I look like or who I date."

Dex let a minute go by before he spoke. "I understand, Sydney. Believe me. But it doesn't change how I feel about you. And I think you feel something for me, too, because you're not the kind of girl who is looking for an easy way to a record deal. Or the kind who gets a thrill out of nailing a celebrity in the back of a tour bus."

He walked to me and stroked my cheek with his thumb. "You're beautiful and intelligent and talented," he whispered.

My breath caught.

"And I want you to have everything you deserve." He swallowed. "I won't get in the way of that. If you think that having something with me will ruin everything else for you, I'll go and not bother you again." He smiled and traced my bottom lip with his thumb. "No matter how much I want to."

He waited for me to tell him not to go. I closed my eyes and forced myself not to answer.

After a moment, he pulled his hand back.

"Goodbye, Sydney. And good luck. With everything."

I waited until the door closed behind Dex to curl up in a ball on my smelly old couch and let my broken heart bleed.

* * * *

When the phone rang at eight a.m., I knew two things for certain. One, it was Tuesday, and two, my mother was on the other end of the line. I dragged my puffy, tear-swollen eyes open and reached for the phone.

"Hi, Mom."

"You sound awful. Are you sick again?"

I cleared my throat. "No, Mom. We had a gig last night." I wasn't going to tell her I'd spent the night crying over some guy. That would only engender more questions and the goal here was to get off the phone as quickly as possible.

"Oh, that's nice. Did you have a good time?"

"Yeah, it was great." I rubbed my itchy eyes and hoped she didn't ask more questions.

"Sydney, your dad and I have been a little worried about you."

"Really? Why?" I asked, although I was sure I could list the reasons: no boyfriend, no boyfriend, and no boyfriend.

"We saw those magazine pictures, Sydney." She paused. "Well, I did. I didn't think it was something your father should see."

Absolute horror froze any comeback on its way to my lips and I had to force myself to swallow before I could answer. This was my worst nightmare. Total humiliation. "It's not what it looked like."

"I should hope not. The Ladies Auxiliary was shocked. Shocked, Sydney."

Well, that wouldn't take much. They were shocked if a married woman chose to use her own name after taking her vows. Still, I imagine those pictures had well and truly sent some of those proper uptight ladies into a dead faint. I smiled a little at the visual. Hmm, maybe there was a song in there.

"Sorry, Mom." I shifted to the side of the bed. "You don't have to worry about that again." I swallowed. "I'm not seeing the guy anymore."

"That's what I wanted to hear."

"Well, you don't have to worry."

"I *am* worried, Sydney. I'm worried you're not meeting the right kind of young men. All those musician types—they're fun to date, I suppose, but they aren't the marrying kind."

Okay, we'd just skipped ahead. Way ahead. "Maybe *I'm* not the marrying kind."

"Don't be ridiculous."

I could just see her waving her perfectly manicured hand in dismissal.

"That's why I'm here in town."

"What?" I shot up.

"I'm here in Nashville, Sydney. I thought we should have a chat, face to face."

Shit, shit, shit, shit, shit.

"Well, I'm pretty busy this week...."

"I flew all the way down here to see you and you can't even make time for your mother?"

The guilt trip worked. And despite the constant dictates on how I should live my life, I did love my mom and it had been a long time since I'd seen her.

"You're right. Of course I would love to see you. Where are you staying?"

"I'm at the Opryland Hotel. I thought you could meet me for breakfast."

It had been years since I'd eaten this early in the day and after last night's drama, I wasn't sure my stomach could take it. But there was no graceful way to get out of it. "I'll be there in an hour."

After a few parting words, I hung up the phone and got in the shower. The warm water felt good on my face and took some of the kinks out of my back. I scrubbed the light makeup off my face that I hadn't bothered to remove the night before and by the time I got out of the shower, the bathroom was completely steamed up but I felt marginally better.

As I searched my closet for something to wear that my mother would approve of, I realized just how concerned Mom must be to fly down here. I'd lived here for a while now and my parents had never once visited. I'd always gone home if I wanted to see them. She was truly worried and I felt bad about causing that.

At the back of my closet, I found the black slacks and pink sweater set Mom had given me for Christmas, the tags still on them. I grimaced, but put them on anyway, pulled my hair back into a low, sleek ponytail and applied some makeup. I took out the large gold hoop earrings and put in the pair of diamond studs Mom had sent for my birthday and frowned at the unfamiliar reflection of myself in the mirror.

I was ready to meet Mom.

* * * *

Opryland Hotel is truly a wonder. With almost three thousand rooms, atriums, spa, and even an indoor river, the place is an attraction all to itself. But it's huge, and it's easy to get lost once inside, so I was a few minutes late meeting Mom at one of the little restaurants inside the hotel.

She wasn't alone at the table, though, and I was conscious of my out-of-breath state and the job the summer humidity had no doubt done on my hair. I slid into an empty seat next to Mom just as the waitress was setting orange juice in front of her and the other two people already at the table.

"Hi, Mom. Sorry I'm late."

Mom smiled at me, then at our breakfast companions. "Sydney is very punctual normally, aren't you, dear?"

"Yes. Of course," I lied.

"Sydney, I'd like you to meet my good friend, Nancy White."

That name sounded familiar.

"And her son, Gregory."

Oh, yeah. Now I remembered.

"Gregory is a lawyer in Knoxville."

I forced a smile. "Nice to meet you, Gregory," I said. He was seated conveniently next to me and I shook his hand.

"A pleasure," he said, smiling at me. "Mom told me you were lovely and she was right. For once." Gregory winked and I knew I had a co-conspirator.

He was easy on the eyes, too. Tall, with light hair and gorgeous green eyes, I doubted getting a girl to go out with him was an obstacle. I wondered why he'd let his mother drag him here to meet me.

"Yeah, I've heard a lot about you, too," I said, smiling back.

The mothers shared a look and a small smile and sipped their cups of tea.

"Sydney is a singer," Mom said. "She's very good."

Mom had actually never heard me sing except for high school musical productions, but hey, the vote of confidence was nice.

"I'd love to hear you sometime." His smile was warm and genuine and there was no earthly reason I shouldn't give in to Mom's matchmaking efforts and give the guy a shot. Except one.

"I'm playing tonight. Are you going to be in town long?"

"I'm heading back to Knoxville tomorrow morning," Gregory said and seemed disappointed.

"But he's a partner in his firm. No one is going to get upset if he extends his trip another day. Or two." Mrs. White cast a sideways look at my mother and I had to concentrate on not doing the eye roll my mom hated.

"I'm sure Sydney has plans. I don't want to disrupt things for her," Gregory said politely but firmly.

A man who knew how to handle his mother. Maybe I should take lessons.

"Well, I'm just saying," Mrs. White said. "You have that option."

Although I only managed to get down a croissant and a glass of orange juice, the breakfast wasn't nearly as horrifying as I had feared. Gregory was funny and nice and was taking the whole set-up thing rather well. I found myself laughing at his intelligent, semi-sarcastic comments more than once. By the time breakfast was over, the mothers were smiling with the smug I-told-you-I-know-what's-best-for-you look and passing knowing glances to each other.

"Well, Nancy and I are going to do some shopping," my mom said, carefully blotting her mouth with the linen napkin. "Sydney, maybe you can show Gregory a little of the city."

"Yes, Gregory is here often for business," Mrs. White added. "But never for pleasure."

I looked over at Gregory with a barely contained smile.

He returned the grin and shrugged. "Only if Sydney doesn't already have plans."

I could have easily made up something, but Gregory was fun to be around. If I made an excuse and went back to my apartment, I would spend the day wallowing in self pity thinking about you-know-who. Not an appealing option.

"I'm free."

The mothers left with an admonishment to behave, and Gregory and I decided to take a walk through one of the atriums.

Plants and trees and flowers of every imaginable variety fresh from the hotel's private greenhouse filled every space, making walking the stone pathways feel more intimate than it actually was. Sunlight filtered through the soaring glass-domed roof and the gurgle of numerous water features made it feel like strolling though an enchanted garden, only better, since it was air-conditioned.

"So how'd you get roped into this blind date?" I asked him as we walked along, side by side.

"Mom's been pestering me for while to call you," he said. "But I'd put her off. Nothing personal."

"I understand. It seems like your mom and mine are two peas in a pod."

"Yeah. Seems that way. Sorry about the ambush date thing," he said, smiling. "If I'd known they planned to spring it on you, I would have made some excuse. Or at least called to warn you."

"Thanks." I shrugged. "But I wasn't doing anything today anyway. And this hasn't been bad."

"No. Not bad at all." We stopped on an arched bridge, overlooking a small pond surrounded by more plants and flowers, and leaned against the railing. "Maybe mothers really do know best. Once in a while." He looked at me and smiled. "I like you."

I could tell he did. If I had met him under different circumstances, I might have pursued something with him. But as it was, my heart was still aching for just one person. The wrong person.

"I like you, too, Gregory, but –"

"But you don't want to go out with a guy your mom set you up with?"

"No, it's not that. I…there's someone else." I looked away. "Or was."

"Ah, I see. Bad timing, then."

"Yeah. Horrible. You're a really nice guy, though."

"It's okay. You don't have to explain, Sydney."

I looked back at him. He was smiling again, a lock of blond hair falling over his forehead. He was perfect. Funny, smart, successful, and most definitely hot. He was the kind of guy a girl would end up in the society pages with, instead of a seedy tabloid. But I just couldn't think about someone else. Not yet. It was all still too raw.

"You're still welcome to come to the show tonight," I said. "If you want to."

"I'd love to hear you sing. But I don't want to give Mom false hopes for a proposal and grandchildren." He smiled and straightened. "Here," he said, pulling a business card from his jacket pocket. "My card. I really did have fun this morning. And I'd love to spend more time with you, sometime. If things change…well, keep me in mind, okay?"

I took the card he offered and stared at it for a minute before putting it in my purse. "Okay."

"I am actually here on business often, like Mom said. We could, I don't know, have dinner or something."

"We can do that even if things don't change, Gregory." I said. "Just as friends." I leaned in close and whispered, "The moms don't even have to know."

"That sounds great. And it's Greg. I hate 'Gregory.'"

We met up with the mothers a little while later, when Greg had a sudden "emergency" that required him to head back to Knoxville right away. So with a hug and a wink, he ushered his mother into his black BMW and headed out the hotel's circular drive. Which left me alone with Mom.

"It's too bad Gregory had to go back," Mom said, frowning. "It seemed like you two hit it off."

"Yeah. We did. Maybe another time."

We walked back inside to the atrium and sat down on a park bench along one of the walkways.

"You didn't like him."

"No, I really did," I said honestly. "It's just...."

"That musician you were in the photos with," Mom finished. There was a disappointed look in her eye when she turned to me.

"Yeah," I breathed. "Dex." Just saying his name hurt. "But I'm not seeing him anymore."

Mom surprised me then. "Why not?"

"What?"

It's clear you really like this guy, Sydney." She took a deep breath, then leveled her gaze on me. "I'm still your mother and I know when my baby girl is hurting."

I looked at my hands, willing my eyes not to tear up again. "It would never work between us."

"Why not?"

Then the whole thing came tumbling out. Every reason I'd given myself. Every reason I'd given Dex. "Because he's a big star. And there are always a lot of bimbos around. And because of those horrible pictures." I looked into Mom's blue eyes, a carbon copy of my own. "Because I want to be more than some man's wife."

Mom looked away and I was afraid I'd hurt her feelings. "You don't want to be me," she said, and I realized she was more percep-tive than I'd ever given her credit for.

"I love you, Mom. And I respect what you've done. I just...want something different."

She was quiet for a minute and I was just about to open my mouth and apologize all over the place. Maybe claim a drug addiction. Any reason to backtrack on what I'd said. But Mom spoke first.

"I know, Sydney. And I've always respected you for that."

"Huh?" Aliens had kidnapped my real mother, I was sure. The one who bought me sweater sets and whose entire life revolved around the Ladies' Auxiliary.

"You're so strong, Sydney. Stronger than I ever was. You know what you want and you're going for it." She gave me a smile and patted my leg. "I know it's been harder than you let on. And I'm proud of you for keeping with this music thing of yours. For not giving up. I probably don't tell you that enough."

Tears threatened again, but this time it was happy tears, and I hugged my Mom.

"My dearest wish in life is to see you happy, Sydney." She stroked my hair back from my face as she had when I was a child. "You've been fearless in going after whatever you wanted. If this man is what you want, then go after him. Figure out a way to sort through all the crap and make it work."

I did cry then. Right there on my mother's shoulder in the middle of the atrium, like I was fifteen years old again and suffering my first broken heart.

"I wish I could, Mom. I just don't see a way."

Chapter Nine

"I CAN'T believe you dumped Dex Wilder," Becca said as we cleared the last table of beer bottles, cocktail napkins, and half-eaten crab cakes. "You've clearly lost your mind."

I tugged at the rented poodle skirt that was about a size too big and picked up the tray full of garbage. At least the saddle shoes were comfy and it was nice having my hair up off my neck in a high, bouncy '50s style ponytail. I headed towards the kitchen area of VFW hall where we'd just waited on about sixty Korean War veterans during their annual dinner reunion. "I didn't dump him. We were never together." Not really.

"Uh-huh. That's not the picture I remember seeing on the cover of *The Rag*."

"Sex together and together-together are two different things, Becca."

"I know. I just thought. Well, it seemed like you two had more than just a hook-up going on."

"Well, we didn't."

She knew I was lying and I could tell she wanted to say something else, but after all the emotional stuff with my mom a few days earlier, I just wasn't in the mood to go there again.

Becca started to speak, but Ricky came in and she went to work unloading the garbage and putting the glasses in the sink.

"Good job tonight, girls," he said, pulling out a wad of cash, presumably from the tip jar. Ricky tended bar at some of the gigs to cut costs and usually shared the take with us.

He split the cash in half and handed us each a handful of ones. "You girls worked your tails off tonight and everybody said what a great shindig it was, even shorthanded as we were."

"Thanks, Ricky. That's sweet." I took the money and stuck it in my pocket.

"I hope you're not going to quit on me now that you've got your rich boy toy," he said grinning at me.

"Oh, I wouldn't go there," Becca said, tucking her half of the cash in her bra.

"It's okay, Becca." I turned back to Ricky. "No danger there. Don't worry. I'll be lugging trays and cleaning up beer until I'm eighty."

"Good," Ricky said, patting my shoulder. "You girls need a ride home?"

"No, but thanks," I said. "I drove."

I hadn't been to the apartment all day and when I checked the mail, there was an official-looking envelope mixed in with the stack of bills and pizza coupons that choked our mailbox.

A record label's name and address was printed in the corner and at first I thought it was another rejection. Definitely not what I needed tonight.

But then I noticed the handwriting on the address. Dex's handwriting.

"Anything good?" Becca asked, coming up the stairs behind me. I shoved the letter under some other mail and smiled. "Nope, not unless we need replacement windows at the lowest price of the season."

She went inside and dropped her stuff on the floor. I followed but went straight to my room. "I'm hitting the sack."

"See you in the morning," she said, settling into the couch cushions with a bag of Doritos.

I sat on my bed and stared at the envelope for a full five minutes, a range of emotions coursing through my body, making my fingers tremble. Excitement. Disappointment. Pain. Hope.

I ripped open the flap and pulled out the letter. Two tickets fell into my lap, but I didn't bother to look at them. I unfolded the letter.

Sydney,

I've been invited to perform at the Opry Saturday night. I know I said I'd leave you alone but I can't stop thinking about you. It would mean a lot to me if you were there.

Love,

Dex

It was short, but I could feel the sincerity in every word. And that one four-letter word before his name. I'd never heard him use it before. It sent my heart tripping, and even though I knew it was a sentiment I could easily share if I let myself, I couldn't go there. I just couldn't. I picked up the tickets and stared at them for a moment.

I wanted to go. And I didn't. And I did.

I could feel Dex's emotions though his short note. His excitement about finally being taken seriously as a performer worthy to grace the Opry's stage. I knew that feeling. How could I say no? But how could I say yes if I ever expected to put my feelings for him and our impossible potential relationship behind me? I couldn't. But I couldn't let him down, either. This would be it. Our final meeting. I'd watch from the audience, then go home and forget all about Dex Wilder. For good.

I picked up the tickets and went to my bedroom door.

"Hey Becca? What are you doing Saturday night?"

* * * *

The Opry was usually staged in a specially constructed theatre on the grounds of the Opryland Hotel and the Opry Mills Mall. But a few times a year, when the newer venue was being used for something else, the Opry came home to the Ryman. Tonight was one of those nights and the theatre was filled to capacity.

The auditorium seemed intimidating to me when it was empty. Now, with 2,300 people filling the seats, I couldn't imagine performing on the stage without puking my guts out beforehand.

The energy of the audience was nearly tangible. People from all walks of life, from tourists to locals, celebrities to nobodies, rich to just making it, sat side by side in the antique church pews filling the hall. People wore everything from formal dress, to jeans, to full-on country-western costumes. It was as diverse and as varied a crowd as you could imagine, but they were all there for one reason. The music. It was all about the music here.

Becca and I had good seats on the bottom level, right on the center aisle. We were close enough to the stage to see the sweat on the performers' brows, but not so close we had to crane our necks to do so.

We got there well before the opening act and I couldn't help but wonder if Dex was nervous. He'd performed hundreds of shows in front of large crowds. But the Opry was special, and I imagined an artist's first performance there was like losing his virginity. It symbolized not just record sales or radio air play or concert ticket sales, but true acceptance as an artist. Dex had topped the charts for two years and only just now had been invited to perform at the Opry.

It was a big night for Dex and I was honored he'd wanted me to be there, even if I still wasn't sure I should be.

"Did you see who is sitting two rows behind us?" Becca whispered.

I turned casually and glanced back. "George Straight," I whispered.

"I don't care how old he is. He's hot." She smiled over her shoulder at the poor man and his wife.

I'd spotted several big-time country stars in attendance tonight, but was trying not to be a total fan-girl about it. That wasn't the Nashville way. People treated celebrities just like the neighbors they were, and even though I was a transplant from the Midwest, I got it.

"Knock it off, Becca. He's married."

The lights blinked and went down and the emcee came out to greet the crowd.

My palms were sweating and I could barely sit still in my seat, waiting to see him. Dex, on stage.

There were several acts before him, though I couldn't have told you who they were. All I could think about was Dex.

Finally the emcee introduced him.

"And making his first Opry appearance, a man who needs no introduction. Double-platinum recording artist and CMA's entertainer of the year, Dex Wilder!"

The crowd applauded and my heart beat a pounding rhythm in my chest. When Dex walked out, it nearly stopped.

Dex wore his signature black cowboy hat, dark jeans, and black boots. His face was clean shaven, though, and under the lights, the planes and valleys of his face were even more pronounced. He flashed the crowd a winning smile while he adjusted the mic stand, then bid everyone good evening.

He sat on the stool in the middle of the stage by himself and the lights dimmed, except for a small spotlight on Dex. His guitar was cradled in his lap and he propped one booted foot on the rung of the stool.

Dex was so handsome he took my breath away. He was every cowboy fantasy I'd ever had, but better. Because I knew he was real. He had that unusual kind of magnetism really stellar performers have, but that wasn't the only reason I couldn't take my eyes off him.

His being alone on the stage wasn't his usual set-up. His big, loud party songs usually boasted the full back-up band, complete with electric guitars, drums and sometimes a banjo or violin And scantily clad backup singers, of course. They were almost as famous as Dex himself, kind of like the Dallas Cowboy cheerleaders. But tonight it was just Dex and his guitar.

When he flashed a nervous smile, I suddenly knew what he was about to do.

"No," I whispered.

"What's wrong?" Becca asked.

"He's going to blow his contract," I said.

"What?"

"Just listen."

My hands were clamped together, white-knuckled in my lap, and I knew I was chewing every bit of lip gloss off my lips.

Dex strummed a few times, the beginning of the familiar melody spilling out. *Nerves*, I thought. *He's nervous.*

Dex looked up and addressed the crowd again. "I know you folks expect a party song from me tonight, but tonight I'd thought I'd do something a little different. This is something I've been working on with a very talented new songwriter," Dex looked straight at me and my breath caught. "And someone who is very special to me." He nodded. "Thanks for being here, Syd."

I smiled weakly and nodded back. Hundreds of eyes went to me, but I only had eyes for Dex.

He smiled at me and turned his attention to the guitar.

The melody came easily and sure to his fingers. He'd been practicing and knew the tune by heart. I could hear the crowd behind me whispering, a little confused but curious as to what the hell Dex was doing. I didn't see his manager or producer, but I was sure if they were here, or at home listening to the broadcast, they were about to pop something.

What the heck was Dex doing? He had a successful career. Made lots of money. So he did shallow little party songs. There were hundreds of musicians in Nashville probably listening to the show right now who would kill to have the career Dex had, and here he was, willing to throw it all away.

To risk everything.

For something he believed in.

Something he loved.

A wave of warmth spread over me and I realized I was looking at the bravest man I'd even known.

The notes echoed through the auditorium, low and sweet and thready at first, building to a stronger line as his rich baritone blended with the music and the lyrics perfectly.

With every note he sang, I could feel the crowd's growing awe. Dex was good. He truly had talent and charisma knew how to use it. And he was risking everything to show people what he could do.

Shivers ran though me as I heard my words – our words – the lyrics we'd written at his house that night, spill elegantly from his mouth. If I closed my eyes, I could almost imagine he was singing just for me, that we were alone. That the night had ended differently than it had that awful morning.

He sang the two verses we wrote, then played a bridge I hadn't heard before. I opened my eyes and stared at him. It was perfect. Then he launched into the third verse.

He looked directly at me now and I could feel thousands of eyes on me, gauging my reaction. Gauging his.

The song was about the rush of a first love, first attraction that consumed him. But the third verse was about something deeper. How the emotion had crept up on him until he could think of nothing else. Until he'd fallen in love totally unexpectedly. It was about us.

The song ended on a hopeful note, the narrator wanting to know if the woman he adored felt the same way.

I swallowed. And smiled weakly.

The final notes of the song wound out sweet yet hopeful, echoing throughout the completely silent auditorium.

I held my breath. Would it be well received, or would Dex be basically blackballed from performing the music he'd chosen? Would the fans let him change or would his career end right there?

There was a shocked lull.

Then the place went wild.

Twenty-three hundred pairs of feet hit the floor simultaneously as the entire auditorium stood and clapped and cheered for Dex.

He looked a little shocked at first, then smiled. Bigger than I'd ever seen him smile before.

"Are you okay?" Becca shouted into my ear and it was then I realized tears were streaming down my face.

I wiped them away. "Yeah."

Dex had risked it all for what he wanted. Professionally and even personally with me when he told me how he felt. He'd taken a chance. Rolled the dice. Risked everything he'd worked so hard to build.

And what about me? I was afraid of a tabloid photo and a few backhanded remarks? It seemed silly now as I stood looking up at Dex, the man I knew I'd come to love for his honesty and his bravery and his good heart. To risk a couple of bad photos for the man looking down at me with so much love in his eyes. I had been a fool. A complete idiot. So what if people said I'd got what I'd gotten because of Dex? That made me want to try that much harder to prove myself. I just hoped it wasn't too late.

I slid out of the seat and hurried up the aisle.

Dex was still at the mic thanking everyone. Everyone was still cheering and clapping and yee-hawing. The sound was deafening. And heavenly.

I hurried up the aisle, Becca right behind me, and headed for the backstage area as I heard Dex tell everyone goodnight.

His was the last act of the night and I couldn't wait one more second to see him. To touch him. To tell him everything that had hit me like a ton of bricks only moments before.

I loved him. And I had to tell him so. Immediately, if not sooner.

It took us a few frustrating minutes to find our way through the maze that lead to the dressing rooms. The narrow corridors were clogged with performers and people carrying instruments and equipment. But at last we reached the dressing rooms and found the one with Dex's name on it.

Dex's head of security, the one who had put me in handcuffs the first time I'd crashed Dex's dressing room, stood sentinel outside his door again. But this time I had Becca.

"You can't go in there, Miss –" he narrowed his eyes. "Oh, it's you."

He radioed for backup and pulled his handcuffs off his belt. "You're not getting by me again, Missy."

I crouched, too, ready to do whatever was necessary to get to Dex. "Oh yes, I am."

Suddenly a banshee whoop pierced the air and Becca launched herself at the guard.

I ran past him and into Dex's dressing room, slamming the door behind me.

I leaned against the door, panting. I heard Becca's yells as she was carted away and I smiled. I'd be bailing her out in an hour, I was sure.

"You came."

Dex had walked out of the bathroom, toweling his sweaty hair. And when he saw me, his whole face lit up.

I brushed my hair out of my face and walked over to him.

"Yeah. I came."

"I'm glad." He slung the towel around his neck and gripped the ends with white-knuckled hands.

We started to speak at the same time.

"Go ahead," he said, looking down at me. I could feel the intensity of his gaze on me, his body heat. But the look he gave me, one of so much hope and love was what sent my pulse skyward this time.

"You were amazing."

I shook my head when he tried to speak. "No. Truly amazing. The performance, yeah, but just your pure courage. To put it all on the line." I shook my head. "You're amazing."

"Or amazingly stupid."

I moved towards him until my neck was tilted way back and his lips were only a few inches from mine.

His hands dropped from the towel to my shoulders.

"You're pretty amazing, too," he said. There was a sad note in his voice. "I know I said I'd leave you alone –"

That was when I rose up on my tiptoes and kissed him. I wrapped my arms around his neck and put everything I was thinking and feeling into that one kiss.

And when we broke apart, he was smiling.

"Does this mean—"

I kissed him again and there were no more questions.

He leaned in and kissed me back, uncertainty gone, leaving only Dex and me and the passion that ran hot between us from the first time we met.

Just as I was really getting into the kiss, the dressing room door burst open and a cluster of men all talking excitedly at once flooded the small space.

Dex broke the kiss and glared at them.

It was his manager, his publicist, his agent, his producer, and the president of his record label. They all looked like carbon copies of each other. Short, balding, dressed in dark slacks and blue button-up shirts with sports coats.

"No, if we market him as a singer-songwriter, we can get more mileage," his agent was saying. "And think about the royalties."

"The test came back negative," said his publicist. "He's not the daddy."

"Let him be the singing cowboy. A balladeer," said the producer.

"I want him in the studio first thing in the morning," said the president of the record label. "We're going to release this as a single on Monday."

"Get out," Dex shouted over the top of them all. "Now."

He literally shoved all of them into the corridor. To the security guard standing outside, he said. "Don't let anyone else in tonight. Understand?"

"Yes, Mr. Wilder. Sure thing."

Dex slammed the door and turned the lock.

I was laughing. "Dex. You're going to get in trouble. Those were important people."

He shook his head. "No. You're important people."

A shiver ran up my spine as he stalked towards me his eyes gone dark and deliciously dangerous. "And you're mine."

He leaned in and kissed me almost sweetly.

"Let's go home."

Chapter Ten

FLASH BULBS greeted us when we emerged from Dex's dressing room, but this time I hardly noticed. My body hummed with awareness and I could hardly wait to get back to the house. The security guard cleared a path for us and we made out way to a waiting car parked out back of the auditorium.

Somehow, we managed to restrain ourselves until we drove through the gates of his home. We managed to keep most of our clothes on until Dex shut the front door behind us. We managed to keep from touching each other until we were finally alone in his bedroom. And then we didn't.

Dex unbuttoned most of the buttons on his shirt before, with growing impatience, he ripped it the rest of the way off. Buttons flew across the room and clattered on the floor.

I giggled and worked on my own buttons.

He jerked his white T-shirt over his head and went to work on his fly with a mischievous look in his eye.

"Funny, is it?" he asked me, approaching.

I kicked off my shoes and shimmied out of my dress.

His breath caught. I guess he liked my black g-string-and-bra set.

He was down to his boxer-briefs with his pants pooled around his bare feet. And all he could do was stare at me.

I gave him the sauciest grin I could muster and sauntered over to him.

Tracing a finger down the center of his chest, I looked up at him through lowered lashes.

"You like?"

The way his shorts were bowed out said "yes".

I stroked my hands down his hard torso, over the twin rows of muscles that stippled his torso and lower to the waistband of his briefs.

He reached for me, but I danced out of his way. "Uh-uh. My turn."

"Sydney." There was a warning in his voice, a barely constrained violence that sent erotic shivers tripping up my spine.

"No touching until I say, okay?"

"You're killing me here."

I smiled. "I know."

His hands fisted at his sides, but he complied. I went to my knees and tugged down his underwear until I could see all that magnificent male, just waiting for me. I licked my lips and went to my knees.

All of our previous encounters had burned hot and fast. There had been no time to savor, no time to explore. I planned to remedy that this go-round.

I slid Dex's underwear down his lightly furred legs and he stepped out of them. At last he was standing before me completely naked. I looked up to find him staring down at me with naked lust and something else burning in his gaze.

I smiled and ran my hand over him.

His eyes closed and his mouth opened. I could feel his muscles tense but he kept his promise. He didn't touch me.

I stroked his legs, moving my hands around to his backside and gave a little squeeze, then pulled him towards me so I could finally taste him.

I took him into my mouth, tasting heat and salt and male. All Dex. He groaned deep in his throat and jerked forward slightly, giving me a jolt of feminine satisfaction. I loved the fact that I was giving him so much pleasure.

It was giving me pleasure, too. Blood coursed though my body in a torrent and the tiny silk swath between my legs was growing wetter with each passing moment.

"Sydney. I can't – " He gasped.

I stood up on tiptoes to kiss him fully and deeply, then pulled back to simply gaze at him.

Dex's eyes blazed dark with passion. Sweat beaded on his brow and he was visibly shaking.

Then I was crushed against his burning chest, his arms wrapped around me like a vise. His mouth was on my throat and we were moving. Backwards, backwards, until my legs hit the edge of the bed and then we were falling.

He landed half on me, his mouth already on mine, his hands tangled in my hair.

I wrapped my arms around his neck and kissed him back. His thigh was between mine, rubbing at the silk there. I loved the feel of the light hair on his legs rasping against my bare skin and arched into him for even more contact.

He moved his mouth to my throat and kissed a line down over my collarbone, down to the valley between my breasts.

"As much as I love this, it has to go," he said, nuzzling my lacy black bra. I untangled my arms long enough to reach behind me and unhook the thing.

By the time he slid the wisp of silk down my arms, my breasts were aching for a little attention. He tossed the bra over his shoulder and propped his head on one elbow.

"You're gorgeous. Perfect."

He used a fingertip to stroke me with a whisper-soft touch that had me biting my lip.

"Dex…."

"Oh, who's getting a little eager, now? Can't take the teasing, huh?"

He moved to the other breast and traced it just as slowly, driving me wild. My hands fisted at my sides and my breath came in breathy little gasps. "Please."

"Please what?"

I didn't know how he could exercise such control when I was burning up inside. How was this not killing him, too?

"Touch me," I said. "Put your mouth on me. Love me."

I rolled towards him and put my hands on his chest, lifting my swollen lips for his kiss.

Dex gathered me into his arms and kissed me slowly and deeply, with near reverence. His hand traced the curve of my bare shoulder, down my arm to the curve of my hip, leaving goose bumps in his wake.

He slipped a finger beneath the string of my panties and tugged. I shifted to allow him to remove them completely and then we were pressed together, full on, skin on skin. I burrowed into him, craving as much contact as humanly possible.

His hand caressed the indentation of my hip and lower to my thigh. He hitched my thigh over his hip and suddenly I was completely open to his caress.

I gasped.

"Okay, babe?" he whispered against my lips.

"Oh, yeah."

He gazed at me, a small smile playing at he corners of his red-dened lips. I was close enough to see the flecks of ebony in his eyes. To count his eyelashes, if I wanted to. To see clearly the emotions playing themselves out there, totally open, totally honest.

He slid his hand over my backside to tease me with the same whisper touch that drove me out of my mind. His erection throbbed against my belly and I jerked instinctively towards him.

"Easy, babe. We've got all night," he said. "And every night."

He slipped his fingers between my thighs then, caressing me with gentle pressure. He dipped his head for another sweet kiss and slipped one long finger inside me.

I groaned into his mouth at the first sweet penetration. But it was only a fraction of what I really wanted. What I needed. His thumb slid up and I nearly came off the bed.

He chuckled low in his throat. "Easy, babe," he repeated. "I've got you."

Kissing my throat, he slid lower on my body, all the while his finger and thumb continuing their slow teasing.

Dex nudged me to my back and moved even lower, pressing kisses across my collarbone. His fingers moved in and out of my body in a slow, slick slide and I was sure he could feel the way my pulse went wild under his intimate caress.

Dex cupped my breast, rubbing his thumb over the swollen peak before dipping his head for a taste.

The sensation of his rough tongue had me writhing in the silk sheets. I grasped at his hair, but he quickly caught my wrists in his hand and pinned them to the bed over my head, then went back to the work of driving me out of my mind.

Finally he released my wrists and withdrew his fingers from my body. I groaned in protest, feeling suddenly empty and needy.

He grinned at me and shifted off the foot of the bed completely. He grasped my thighs and tugged until I was at the edge of the bed, too, then went down on his knees on the floor hooked my knees over his shoulders so he could put his mouth right where I ached the most.

He loved me gently at first, then with more pressure. His hand caressed my thighs, turning them into jelly.

I was on fire and I didn't know how much more I could take before I burst into flames. Still, Dex took his time.

At last, he raised his head. "You are so beautiful, Sydney, so sexy. And all mine."

"Dex," I breathed. "Please. I need you."

"That's what I was waiting to hear, babe."

He surged to his feet and bringing my legs up until my feet were next to his ears, aligned himself to my opening.

He eased in slowly. Too slowly, and I bunched the comforter in my sweaty fists, gritting my teeth all during the long, slow slide home.

He filled me completely, touching every place, every nerve I needed him to. The delicious sense of fullness, of completeness, flooded my senses. I felt my muscles clench around him, needing him to move, needing him to stay right where he was.

"God," he breathed. "You're perfect. Absolutely perfect."

He moved then, slowly drawing himself all the way out, then sliding back home until his pelvis ground against mine.

"You feel so good, Syd. This was all I could think about these past weeks."

He pulled out again in agonizing slowness.

"Seeing you like this. So hot, so sweet at the same time."

He slid back inside, slick and hot and wet.

"So open to me. To us."

He pulled out a little faster now.

"To have you here, all to myself."

He drove home.

"All mine."

Dex turned his mouth to press a wet kiss to the arch of my foot, then dropped my legs, leaned forward and moved us both further up the bed.

His chest came down on mine in comforting, satisfying weight, and my legs instinctively wrapped around his waist to bring him even closer. He pressed his face in the crook of my neck and, gathering me closer, began to move.

The sweet friction built and built as his breath rasped out, tickling the flesh of my throat. I buried my hands in his hair and gave over to the sensation, letting the last barriers between us crash down.

He drove onto me faster and harder until it seemed every nerve in my body was focused on that point, on our connection. On the sweet sensation of his sliding in and out of my body bringing us so much pleasure I thought I'd explode from the pure joy if it.

Finally, he raised his head and cradling my head in his big, warm hands, brought my mouth to his for a quick, sweet kiss.

"I love you, Syd. You know that, right?"

I arched up, needing just that little push over the edge, I gritted my teeth and he thrust one more time, hard, as something burst inside me, sending waves of hot swift pleasure flooding everything inside. My heart, my mind, my body shuddered in response. I could feel his answering shudder deep inside and grasped at his forearms to keep us both from being swept completely away.

My breath was ripped away as the final clench and a shudder wracked my body and I went limp, sighing his name.

He collapsed on top of me, too, breathing heavy, his skin slick and hot from the exertion. He rolled us back to our sides, keeping the connection, and I threw my thigh over his. Hugging me close, he pressed a kiss to the top of my damp head.

I nuzzled into his chest, listing to his heartbeat. When we were both almost back to normal cardiac rhythms, he began to hum softly in my ear.

I listened for a moment. "What's that?"

"Something new I'm working on."

"I like it."

"You should. It's about you. About us. About this moment." He swallowed. "I'm glad you came tonight."

I smiled up at him. "Me, too." I tightened my leg on his hip.

"That, too." He smiled. "But I meant to the show. I didn't know if you would."

"I didn't know, either." I rubbed small circles into his chest. "I convinced myself it was a bad idea."

"What changed your mind?"

I shrugged lightly. "I couldn't stay away." I pushed at his chest until he rolled to his back, our bodies still connected. I straddled his hips and smiled down at him. "You're growing on me."

Dex flashed my favorite bad boy grin. "That's a fact." He grasped my hips lightly, but kept me from moving, when I would have.

The smile faded and was replaced with a more serious gaze. "I need to know you're going to be here in the morning, Sydney. I think you know I want this to be more than just physical."

"Oh really?" I shifted my hips, but his hand clamped down on my hip, stopping me.

It was time to 'fess up.

"I'm serious, Sydney. I need to know this means something to you."

I calmed the butterflies hatching in my belly and leaned low over his chest. I kissed his lips once, sweetly.

"When I saw you up on stage tonight, for the first time I didn't see Dex Wilder. I didn't see just another guy. I saw you. I saw your courage. Your goodness. Your love. I knew that I couldn't lie to myself anymore. I had to admit that I loved you and find the courage to let you know, too."

His grin broke out and he hugged me to him. "That's what I wanted to hear."

The kiss changed to a slow caress, mingling tongues and lips and breath until heat began to build all over again in the body I was sure had been exhausted.

He broke away and framed my head in his big hands.

"I love you, Syd. That's what matters most to me. We'll figure all the rest out."

I turned my head and kissed his fingers.

"I know we will, Dex. Together."

Epilogue

Three years later

The Tennessean, April 17:

PLATINUM RECORDING artist of hit songs *Don't Walk Away* and *Baby, I Know*, Dex Wilder, and his wife, Grammy-award winning lyricist Sydney Stratton-Wilder welcomed a daughter, Rachael Sydney Wilder, on Tuesday. Mr. Wilder was invited to join the Opry last month. He said although it was an honor, the joy didn't hold a candle to spending time at home with his wife and children. Baby Rachael joins the Wilders' adopted children, Mr. Wilder's niece and nephews, at their Brentwood home.

THE END